About the author:

Kathryn O'Neal trained as a journalist and worked for several years on a number of UK publications. She then moved into teaching and has written several books for her primary school classes over the years.

She has three grown-up daughters, lives in Berkshire and enjoys gardening, reading and campaigning on environmental issues.

D1740096

This book is dedicated to the wonderful children who have inspired me to write – particularly the children of Trinity St Stephen First School in Windsor.

Also my wonderful book club who chose *Eddie* as one of our monthly reads and who were all so supportive in their love of this story.

Thanks to my children Emma, Yasmin and Jessica, who all encouraged me to realise my dream and get this published.

Last, but not least, my husband, Dennis, who helped developed the idea for this story over several years and many cups of tea!

CONTENTS

TIME'S RUNNING OUT FOR EDDIE WATSON

By Kathryn O'Neal

PROLOGUE

A pair of children, one with a long, white smock, hanging to almost her ankles and the other with knee-length, grey shorts and a bright red jumper, huddle over a patch in the soil. They look around and whisper anxiously.

The boy sits back on his black leather shoes and looks up at the oak tree, which looms over them. The girl, frowning as she coughs quietly, turns her head to see what he is looking at and nods briefly before tapping at the soil with a flat stone. The boy then leans forward and their heads almost touch as they energetically dig into the black, stony earth. Soil flies up around them in little puffs as they work away, one of them glancing behind them every few seconds as if fearful of something – or someone.

Eventually they create a little hole in the soil deep enough to satisfy their secret mission. As they both rapidly scan around one last time, the girl pulls, from under her smock, a silver metal box. She rattles it gently at the boy and he allows a smile to pass across his face. Carefully, he takes it from her hands and pushes it deep into the earth, before they both scoop up the soil that is scattered around, and press it over the top of the little hill, pushing the blackness down hard on top of the metal box.

When they finish, there is just a tiny mound to betray their efforts. They take it in turns to stamp hard on it – her with her brown, battered boots and he with his shiny, black shoes which are now speckled with earth. They scuttle about, grabbing small stones to sprinkle on top of the bare soil, and soon it looks as if no one had ever disturbed the flattened ground.

They stand and face each other. The girl coughs again, holding her hand to her chest. He touches her arm as tiny beads of sweat shimmer on her skin. She is thin and quite pale, although a tint of red flushes across her cheeks. He looks at her through his long, dark fringe, which skims low over his eyes. They both gaze up together now into the green leaves of the oak tree, which are dancing lightly in the breeze as if rustling a message across the stories of time.

The boy and the girl both smile as if pleased with themselves and briefly hold hands before turning, and walking away in opposite directions.

CHAPTER 1

Eddie noticed the door on his first day at his new school. He didn't know why, but it seemed to hold a strange attraction for him. As he had walked down the narrow corridor, full of coats, boots, PE kits and battered school bags, he had felt a strange force almost pulling him towards it.

His new headteacher was called Mr Evans and he seemed friendly enough, although Eddie felt a ripple of irritation coming from the teacher as he tripped slightly over a bag left discarded in the middle of the walkway.

"I hope you will remember to put your bag away properly," he muttered to Eddie as he steadied himself against the wall.

There was not much space, as coat hooks seemed to be plastered over the corridor like a flock of unruly birds. Eddie didn't know what to say and soon realised he wasn't really supposed to say anything. He just slumped his shoulders down further, and lowered his head so that his long, brown fringe fell further over his face, shielding his eyes.

As the headteacher carried on explaining details about the school day, Eddie saw the door crouching between the rows of hooks as if trying to hide itself away. There was nothing extraordinary about it except it seemed to generate a strange magnetic force, which almost dragged his hand towards it.

Eddie tried to control himself. He hauled his bags up over his shoulder. He knew the rules, and he knew how to break them. And he had promised, really promised his mother that he would not get into trouble at this new school. His time at his last school had not ended well. But no one had truly understood why Eddie, who was tall for his age, had been forced to push Liam with such strength. He wasn't to know that Liam would fall over and knock his arm so badly on the wooden play equipment. He shuddered silently as he remembered how his mother had been called up to school ("Oh no, not AGAIN, Eddie") and how furious she was that he had been given a two-day suspension ("But I am BUSY, Eddie. You will simply have to stay at home on your own").

Yes, he was determined that his temper would not get the better of him at this school. He wasn't sure exactly how he was going to do it as sometimes he couldn't help getting really, really angry.

Eddie's mother had told him it was that terrible incident with Liam that had finally made her decide to move to Stoneham Cross from their old house twenty miles away. His mum had said it was "time for both of them to make a new start" somewhere else. He suspected, though, that the man dressed in a suit, who had started a loud and unpleasant conversation with his mother on the doorstep a few days earlier, also had something to do with it all.

Eddie had listened fearfully from the kitchen, his ear pressed to the door, as the man had growled something about "unpaid bills" and "you must cough up or we will take you to court". His mother had looked shaken and upset afterwards, but had refused to discuss it with Eddie, saying it was "none of his business".

When she had announced to him a couple of days later that they were moving, the only reason she gave was that it was time for him to go to a different school, and that their new house was in a small town not too far away. Stoneham Cross. She also made him promise that he would behave this time and try to get on with the other kids. He had promised. He told himself he didn't really care anyway.

Eddie glanced over at the door as Mr Evans stooped to pick up a coat and place it on a spare hook. It was just an ordinary door, brown, with chipped paint and scuffs from where bags had been bashed against it and numerous feet had scuttled past. Eddie's fingers almost twitched with a desire to see what was behind it.

St Paul's Primary School was an old building, with the date 1882 proudly carved in stone over the modern front door. A plastic conservatory-like structure had been built around the entrance to create extra security so that visitors could be held behind a password-coded door for which only the teachers knew the numbers. Eddie had thought the white plastic and glass entrance looked weird next to the brick building with its ages-old date written above. When he was dropped off at the front door by his mum, he found himself wondering how many sad children like him had passed through that entrance over the years. The school was more than one hundred years old. Eddie instinctively started to work out how many years it actually was, but shook the numbers out of his head, reminding himself that he really couldn't be bothered with school stuff. What he really enjoyed was his games console and Youtube. He wanted to be a Youtuber when he grew up. A vlogger. Posting funny videos online watched by thousands of eager followers.

As he walked towards the entrance to his new classroom behind the suited jacket of his headteacher, he comforted himself with the thought that it would be only a few hours before he could get back to his computer and look at the latest Youtube video by super vlogger Trickster.

As Mr Evans' hand stretched out to open the classroom door, Eddie found himself glancing back down the corridor.

A beam of light shone through a window between the classroom and where they were standing, striking the round handle of the door. It gleamed in the glare and Eddie could see a pattern engraved into the metal. He bit his bottom lip, shrugged his shoulders and turned away.

CHAPTER 2

The whole class looked up when Mr Evans entered the room. Dozens of eyes stared as Eddie stood in the doorframe trying to appear confident instead of betraying the nerves he really felt. He dropped his bags onto the floor beside him, peering through his fringe at the many eyes, all looking up at him.

"Mrs Jameson," said Mr Evans. "This is your new pupil, Eddie Watson. He was a little late this morning, so maybe someone could help him sort his bags out?"

Eddie bristled with embarrassment. He had told his mum that he wanted to be early on his first day, but she had overslept and told him that he had to wait until she had put her make-up on before taking him.

"I have got to think about first impressions, Eddie," she had muttered, whilst delving into her make-up bag and applying mascara with her mouth wide open in concentration. He thought it was weird that she spent so long putting on make-up and then threw on her onesie to actually drive to school. Sometimes she was so annoying.

Whilst Mr Evans spoke under his breath to the teacher, Eddie glanced around the classroom. The children all still stared at him and he stiffened, not knowing where to look. The brick walls were covered in displays of writing, ideas for words, paintings and one corner had a small cupboard with a selection of books displayed on little stands. The windows were set high up in the walls and the ceiling had been cut short with polystyrene squares, some of which had brown stains on from where rain had dripped through.

Eddie's eyes darted around the room, trying to take it all in and looking anywhere except at the children all waiting expectantly for him to come and sit down. He noticed in one corner of the room there was a little alcove with shelves on either side. Strangely, there were two doors at the back of the alcove. His eyes looked up. Above one door was written "Boys" in letters carved into a stone. And above the other was written "Girls".

Eddie shrugged to himself and thought that looked a bit mental – why on earth would they have a door for girls and a door for boys? He wondered what joke Trickster would make about that! He couldn't wait to get home and see what funny videos Trickster had posted today.

"Eddie?"

He jumped when he heard his name being called and dragged himself back from his thoughts of Trickster's last Youtube video in which he had demonstrated his latest favourite computer game *Crash or Dash*. God, school was so stupid.

"Eddie," repeated the lady at the front of the class. She smiled and walked towards him. "Welcome to Year 5. I am Mrs Jameson."

So this was his new teacher, he thought. She looked like a teacher, with short, brown hair and the usual teacher clothes. She was smiling, but they all smiled… at the beginning.

"Who would like to show Eddie where to put his stuff?" she asked the class. Nearly every hand shot up, some of them waving fingers in the air in enthusiasm and others making strange little squeaking noises in order to get noticed.

Here we go again, thought Eddie. He reminded himself that he had promised that this time it would be better, this time it would be different.

Alfie Hall was chosen to be Eddie's guide for the day. He was a tall boy with short, dark brown hair and a friendly smile, and he got up quickly to go and help show Eddie where to put his bag. The two boys stepped out into the corridor.

"Have you just moved here?" asked Alfie, as he shut the classroom door.

"Yep," said Eddie, who had picked up his bags and followed his new classmate into the walkway.

"Do you like football?"

"Nope," answered Eddie, a little rudely. He pinched his wrist – remember the promise, he reminded himself.

"Do you like Harry Potter? We are reading The Philospher's Stone in class at the moment. I love it. We went to the Harry Potter Studios last week. It was sick!" said Alfie, hopefully.

"Nope. I don't like reading," muttered Eddie.

"Oh," said Alfie, a little disappointed. "What do you like then?"

"Youtube and my games console," answered Eddie. "And I don't like school."

"Oh," repeated Alfie, a little unsure how to continue. "I like computer games too, but I love school. I actually think I prefer school to holidays. Can you believe that?"

"No, I can't," said Eddie. Alfie's face fell slightly.

"Well, here is a spare peg," said Alfie, pointing to a peg at the end of the row, just before the little brown door. "You can put your stuff there."

Eddie dropped the bags off his shoulder and heaved them onto the peg. He had a strange tingling feeling in his fingers as they brushed against the door. It was almost like a tiny electric shock.

"What's behind there?" he asked Alfie, flicking his hand towards the door.

"I think it's some sort of store room," said the other boy, glancing back at the classroom, eager to get back in and not miss out on what was happening.

"I don't know exactly as we aren't allowed in there. Come on, let's get back as Mrs Jameson can shout a bit if we take too long."

Alfie half jogged back to the classroom and Eddie turned back to the door. He couldn't help himself. He reached out towards the handle, noticing the tiny, dark lines, which raced across the silver surface. His fingers lightly touched it. It was almost as if a spark lit up his body when his skin stroked the metal. He staggered back, glancing quickly at Alfie to make sure he hadn't seen him jump. Alfie was opening the classroom door and then turned his head back, beckoning Eddie to join him.

Eddie strolled slowly towards the classroom, determined to discover what was behind that door. Remember your promise, a voice whispered in his head.

CHAPTER 3

Eddie daydreamed through the first part of the morning. Mrs Jameson went on about additions and times tables until Eddie managed to zone out and slump back in his chair. Maths was so easy, he hardly needed to bother thinking and put little effort into his work. His teacher pursed her lips slightly when Eddie handed her his maths book and she scanned his messy scribbles and crossings out. She seemed to start to say something to him, and Eddie started to mentally prepare some excuses. However, after looking at him for a moment, she seemed to change her mind and took his book from him and placed it with the rest for marking later on.

"Break time!" the teacher called cheerfully. The class scraped back their chairs and stood up as Mrs Jameson reminded Alfie that he was to look after Eddie at break.

The playground was surrounded by modern houses, with a tarmacked area decorated with lines and circles and a wooded space on the side of the school which offered play equipment such as small slides, metal climbing frames and various strange-looking wooden animals. Eddie looked at it all with a sneer on his face, pushing his hands into his pockets and flicking his hair down further over his eyes.

The weather was still warm as September was beginning to fade into Autumn and the trees offered some shade. A tall oak tree soared into the sky, its protective branches reaching out like criss-crossing webs.

Keen to be free from their classrooms, the children ran around, their voices full of shrieks and shouts as they played their games and chatted with friends.

"Are you coming to play football?" Alfie asked Eddie, clearly wanting to join in with the boisterous game that had already started on the tarmac. He ran his hand back through his short hair and he attempted a friendly, encouraging smile.

However, Eddie was definitely not interested in anything like football and, although he had promised his mum to make an effort to get on with the other children, he didn't want to show them that he needed their friendship.

"Nah," answered Eddie, kicking some of the bark chips that were scattered under the trees.

"What do you want to do then?" Alfie tried again. He looked longingly over at the football game once more and some of the boys beckoned them over, clearly happy for Eddie to join in.

"Nothing. You go and play," answered the new boy.

Alfie looked strangely at him and then turned quickly and went to join the others. When he reached them, the boys all gathered around and Eddie could see them talking and looking over at him. After a while, they wandered back to their positions and started charging around after the ball, engrossed in their competition and forgetting the new boy standing on the edge of the playground.

Alone again, thought Eddie. He felt a moment of sadness as he saw the ball flying through the air and the boys pushing and shoving to reach a kick. He took a step towards the game, thinking that maybe he could join in, but then pulled himself back, hanging his shoulders and reminding himself that he liked being alone and didn't need anyone. His friendships never seemed to work out. He would just get through the day until he could go home and retreat into his world of *Crash or Dash* and see what Trickster had been up to today on Youtube.

At the end of the afternoon, the children streamed out from school, eager to get home and have their tea. Eddie's mum turned up late and he had to stand on his own next to Mrs

Jameson for five minutes after everyone else had gone, waiting for her.

"So, Eddie," said Mrs Jameson, looking down at him as they stood together on the emptying playground. "What is your favourite subject at school?"

"Dunno," muttered Eddie, staring down at his feet awkwardly.

"You seemed quite confident in maths today," continued his teacher. "Although your work was very messy."

"Well, that's cos maths is easy," he answered.

"A lot of children don't find maths easy at all," said Mrs Jameson gently. "Maybe it's because you're actually quite good at it."

Eddie didn't answer. He didn't like talking to teachers and was saved by his mother finally arriving in a flurry of apologies.

"I am so sorry," she said, rushing to put her mobile phone back into her bag. "I have just had the most manic day!"

Mrs Jameson smiled at her and pushed Eddie gently forward.

"It's fine – it's the first day," said the teacher, with a touch of warning in her voice. "But it would be good if you could make sure you are on time tomorrow. It's not nice for Eddie to have to stand here by himself, Miss Watson."

"Oh he's OK," laughed his mother. "He's used to me. I am always so disorganised!"

Eddie was cross. She almost seemed to be proud of being late.

Eddie and his mum walked across the tarmac and out onto the road. There were cars everywhere and children still being bundled into seats while parents stood chatting and laughing. Eddie's mum had managed to park her car almost opposite the school and she made sure Eddie looked both ways before they crossed the road.

"Well," she said. "The parking is pretty ridiculous here. I will have to make sure I am late every day. That's how I managed to park so close - someone was leaving just as I arrived."

"Oh mum…" Eddie hesitated. " Please don't do that."

"You'll be fine," she said, as she hunted for her keys in her bag.

"You're a big boy now and you need to think about me some-times."

Eddie's head slumped down as he felt a wave of annoyance. He really didn't want to be the one waiting every day on his own to be picked up. Why couldn't she just arrive at the same time as everyone else? Why was he always different to all the others?

Eddie and his mother had moved into a small house just a five minute drive from the school. They had managed to rent it from a landlord who his mum said "was desperate enough to have tenants on benefits". He hadn't really understood what this meant, but he knew that the house was filthy when they moved in and that his mother had made only a small effort to clean it before giving up, saying: "It will be a complete mess again soon, so what's the point?'

He did, however, have his own room, with his own bed, ward-robe, shelves and small desk. The desk was where his computer held pride of place and next to it was his games console. These two friends were his whole universe.

After pestering his mother to make sure the internet was working, he had quickly set up his computer and console and had delved into his electronic world, while his mum scuttled and rummaged around the house, trying to create some sort of order out of their possessions.

That evening, after Eddie and his mum had finished their quick tea of sausages and chips with baked beans, he sat ab-sorbed in the challenge of reaching the next level of *Crash or Dash* as the electronic glare lit up the bare walls of his room. His pupils grew large as they became one with the flickering anima-tions that dashed across his screen.

Alongside the frantic game, Trickster beamed out from the computer screen, paused mid-action and waiting for the play button to launch Eddie into a world of even greater make-be-lieve. An unreal world that was much, much more exciting than the actual world of everyday.

He finally switched off the screen and rolled himself into his bed, pulling his duvet up around his ears.

Eddie lay in the dark, and found himself thinking about the door and how it seemed to be pulling him towards it, whispering a mysterious message to him as he drifted off to sleep.

CHAPTER 4

There was nothing for breakfast the next morning, as Eddie's mother had forgotten to buy any cereal. Eddie gritted his teeth as he opened the cupboard and saw that it was almost empty. The kitchen was strewn with dirty plates and cutlery from the previous evening and he made small angry fists with his hands.

Why were the cupboards always empty, he furiously muttered to himself? He remembered the man in the dark suit stomping off down the path at their old house and slamming the gate. His mother had shut the front door and turned around slowly as he came out of his hiding place in the kitchen. Her face had been flushed and there were tears in her eyes as she looked at him with a worried glance. His heart had sunk.

And here he was. New house, new school and cupboards still empty, and anxious about being late for school again. Nothing changed.

"Oh baby," she had said as she put on her red lipstick and quickly brushed her hair. "Can't you just finish off the baked beans we started last night?"

Eddie glared at the bowl of cold baked beans that sat sadly next to the sink. He couldn't face them, even though he knew he was hungry.

"I will definitely go shopping today," his mother said as she smacked her lips together. "What do you want? Coco Pops?" Eddie nodded glumly as he pulled on his school coat and grabbed his bag.

"Come on, mum. I hate being late. Everyone stares at me," he pleaded, as she leaned forward into the hallway mirror to check everything was in order.

"All right, all right, don't nag," she answered. Thank goodness she then grasped the car keys from a bowl on the shelf under the mirror. Eddie thought: "I am going to be on time today."

Unfortunately, the trip to school also included a quick visit to the local Tesco Express, just down the main road from the school, to grab some food, including Coco Pops, which Eddie munched on as they dashed to school, and a break-time treat. He knew they were supposed to have a "healthy snack" but his mother bought him a chocolate-covered Kit Kat. He was pleased and thought about what he would say if anyone tried to take it off him.

Eddie arrived a few minutes after the bell had been rung. He felt his face burn as he had to step into the class once more in the full glare of the staring eyes of the other children. He could feel his muscles tense and he wanted them all to look away and ignore him. He couldn't help noticing the concerned glance from his teacher. Eddie felt himself growing hot and his head started to spin as he walked towards his table, clenching his sweaty hands under his sleeves. He knew the warning signs and tried to remember his "strategies" for dealing with them. Counting back from ten, breathing deeply, thinking of a blue sky with a bright yellow sun. All total rubbish of course.

"Hi," said a voice next to him as he slumped down into his chair. Eddie ignored it.

"Is your name Eddie?" the voice continued. "That's two days you've been late. Are you always late?"

"Too many questions," Eddie muttered, hoping the voice would go away and leave him alone.

"You are so rude!"

Eddie turned to see who was attached to the voice and met the eyes of the boy next to him. He had bright red hair and a face full of freckles. A big, smiling mouth with two huge, goofy front teeth, which stood out at an alarming angle.

"Who are you anyway?" asked Eddie, in a not very friendly voice.

"Ethan," said tooth-boy. Eddie smirked and turned away, slumping down even further into his seat.

"And I know that you are Eddie. Do you want to play football with us at break?"

"No," said Eddie, shutting the brief conversation down.

He reminded himself that he liked to be alone, but a little voice fluttered in his head, ringing his promise that he would "try harder" to get on with the other children. Well, maybe he would try tomorrow.

At break time, Eddie hung about in the toilets until all the other children had gone outside. He locked the cubicle door and leaned against the wall until the clattering and chatting had drifted into the distance. Wanting to be alone and not wishing to join in with their games, he had decided to quite simply avoid the other children. It had always been a good strategy.

After a while, he slowly opened the door and peeked around to see if there were any adults patrolling the area. He looked down the jumbled corridor. It was completely empty of people – just the way he liked it. Remembering that his mother had bought him a Kit Kat for break, he crept down the corridor to his bag.

As he got closer, he could feel the strange pull of the brown door almost drag his hand towards it. He got closer and closer and it was almost as if the door was vibrating into his body.

Eddie stood in front of it and looked at the handle with its pattern of lines. He bent down slightly to study it and squinted as he tried to see it in more detail. It was like an egg timer, with sand running from the top to the bottom.

He remembered at his last school, they used one of these when he was gripped by one of his "angry outbursts". The teacher would send him out of the class with the teaching assistant and he would have to sit in the library until the sand had run its way through. His teacher had said the timer ran for five minutes and that he was being given "five minutes to calm down". Those few minutes always seemed to last a lifetime, but even then he would struggle to stop the fury that raced through him like a blazing fire.

However, the timer on this door looked older than the blue plastic one with bright yellow sand that had timed his rejection from the class. This one was decorated with swirls and stars. The top part of the timer was full of sand ready to trickle into the bottom, marking the passing of time.

Eddie felt his hand reach out towards it. He glanced one more time up and down the corridor and turned the handle quickly, opening the door and seeing the darkness within.

Before he knew it, he had stepped in through the door and closed it with a tight bang behind him. He was in complete darkness. Not even a chink of light could be seen and he could feel his heart thumping in his chest like a drum. The beating got louder and louder and his breathing got quicker and quicker. The air seemed to shake around him. He had to get out. Why on earth had he gone in there in the first place?

Eddie fumbled behind himself for the handle, suddenly worried that there was no handle inside the cupboard and he would be locked inside for ever. He felt panic stricken as he managed to find the knob and turn it. Would it open? He rattled it frantically, the sound echoing around like a cat trying to escape.

Suddenly the door flew open and Eddie stumbled backwards into the corridor, breathing the fresh air in deep gulps. Slowly he turned around, scared that he was going to be caught by an adult and find himself in deep trouble.

He could not believe his eyes.

Instead of the bustle of brightly-coloured coats, bags and gym kits, he saw a plain, tiled floor where the carpet had been. Simple, black, old-fashioned hooks had tatty, brown bags thrown over them. Instead of the polystyrene squares, there was a high wooden ceiling that seemed to soar upwards. He looked ahead and there was his classroom with its indoor window looking into the corridor. But instead of the organised clutter of writing, art and words, there was one huge map, a globe and a picture of a stern-looking queen. She must be a queen, as she had a small crown on her head and looked very serious. He stood on tiptoe and, hardly able to breathe, he peered into the room.

On one side of the room, the large interactive whiteboard had been replaced by a blackboard on which someone had written with chalk. He gulped as he saw the letters printed on it with neat, careful writing: September 15th 1898.

CHAPTER 5

Eddie looked anxiously around him. Nothing was exactly the same but also not entirely different. The classroom was there, the corridor was there, the hooks were there, but the details had all changed.

He stared intently into the classroom, feeling his hands begin to shake slightly underneath his sleeves. Instead of the blue tables and bright red chairs, there were wooden desks, which stepped away from the front of the classroom like the seats in a cinema. The tables at the back were higher than those at the front and the desks were in long, straight lines. The desks were packed tightly together and, instead of chairs, there were wooden benches to sit on. In one corner was a heavy metal container with a pipe leading up to the ceiling. It looked like it was some sort of heater.

He had no idea what was happening and suddenly wished he had never touched the strange door and wished he was just a normal boy who enjoyed football at break time rather than wandering around on his own and sneaking into forbidden cupboards.

As he tried to calm his breathing, he could hear the distant sound of children shouting and laughing. He looked behind him at the cupboard door, which stared back at him defiantly. He had no idea what to do. Surely he should grab the handle and try to return to the world as he knew it, but he didn't move.

Suddenly he heard footsteps coming down the corridor and

he made a split second decision to slip into the classroom. He pulled the door open quickly and crawled up between the first row of desks so that he couldn't be seen from the corridor.

Eddie noticed that the room smelt. It was a mixture of sweat, dirty clothes and damp feet and he held his hand to his nose in disgust. The floor was dusty and covered in small blotches of ink. He crawled under the desks to the far end as the distant voices got closer and closer. Glancing back at the bottom part of the door, he crossed his fingers in a desperate hope that the footsteps would not enter the room and find him.

They stopped outside the door and he could hear two women talking. Their voices became clearer and he realised that although they were talking English, their accent was strange and not like anything he had ever heard before.

"All right, Rose," said one of the women. "I will go into the classroom and see if I can find it for you."

"Thank you so much, Kate," was the response. "I would very much appreciate that. The inspector is due next month and I must ensure all the records are entirely up to date."

Eddie heard the handle begin to turn and he stared around in desperation. He then saw the familiar sight of the two doors ahead of him – one with *Boys* and the other with *Girls* written above. He dashed towards them, keeping his head down as he crawled on all fours across the wooden floor (where had the carpet gone?). He reached up, his fingers trembling with fear, and found the handle (he hoped it was the Boys' door) and opened it quickly before tumbling out into the fresh air.

As soon as he was outside, Eddie crouched down to make himself as small as possible. Without thinking, he scuttled along the side of the building and crept around the corner to hide.

He then slowly peered around the corner back into the main playground. His eyes grew wide with astonishment. The playground was full of children, but not children as he knew them. They were dressed strangely and playing with hoops and small balls they were rolling on the ground. Some were just running around throwing their caps at eachother and whooping with laughter. Eddie grasped the side of the brick building, his knuckles white and his mouth open in amazement. What was going on? What was happening? He couldn't tear his eyes away from the sight before him.

"Who are you?" said a quiet voice behind him.

Eddie's blood froze and he turned with a gasp to see who had spoken. It was a girl. She was walking slowly towards him, a confused look on her face. Her brown hair was tied back with a white ribbon and she was wearing an odd, long white apron that covered her dress. She was pale and thin and stopped a little distance away from him, trying to make sense of what she was seeing.

A little crease of concern appeared between her eyes, but she was still and composed in comparison with Eddie's thumping heart and trembling hands. Gently, she reached her hand up to her mouth and coughed a little before repeating: "Who *are* you? What are you doing here?"

"I...I... don't really know," stuttered Eddie, glancing anxiously around him. "I have no idea how I got here."

"What are you *wearing*?" she said, looking him up and down with a frown. "And where's your cap and jacket?"

Eddie looked down at his bright red jumper and realised that there had been nothing like it on the playground he had seen moments before. There had just been black, brown and grey. He must stand out like a red traffic light. The two children stood and stared at eachother, both confused by the appearance of the other person and clearly not knowing what to do next. The girl coughed gently again, her hand reaching to her chest with the effort.

At that moment a shriek announced a group of girls skirting around the corner of the building in a game of chase. Eddie's head whipped around in fear and he flattened himself pointlessly against the wall in to try and avoid being seen. The girl watched her classmates as they laughed and screamed, chasing eachother right past Eddie. One of them reached out and tried to grab another girl's ribbon, laughing as she missed and the girl escaped her clutches.

They came to a halt in front of Eddie and his new companion. They stopped and stared right at them.

"There you are!" said one of them to the girl with the white ribbon. "Are you not coming to play?"

"No, Emily," she answered, looking in confusion back at Eddie. "I am not feeling good today. I just want to… sit alone for a while."

The group of girls scampered off, giggling and laughing as they continued their game of chase into the distance.

The pale girl turned slowly to Eddie.

"Did you see that?" she asked.

"What?" said Eddie, wondering why the girls had not said anything to him, especially as his red jumper must have made him stand out like a beacon.

"They didn't see you. They looked right at you and didn't see you."

CHAPTER 6

Eddie stared hard at the girl. His head was spinning. She stared hard back, a questioning look on her face challenging him to speak. He wondered where on earth he was and what was happening to him.

The girl lifted her hand to her mouth and started to bite her fingernails absent-mindedly as she gazed at the strange boy standing in front of her.

Her confusion over his appearance was obvious from the expression on her face. She looked him up and down, taking in his trousers, which stopped at his knees, and his bright jumper with the school logo sewn into the top corner. Her eyes rested on his bright, black, shiny school shoes with Velcro fastenings. She then held out one of her own feet, encased in brown leather. The sole was worn and the laces frayed. Her stare moved back from her boots to his shoes, as if trying to work out why his footware was so different from hers.

She slowly looked up from her boots towards his face, still nibbling at her fingers in puzzlement.

"Can you help me?" Eddie said, as he looked around anxiously. "I have no idea what is happening. One minute I was at school, the next minute I was here.... Well, still at school, but not MY school. And I have no idea why you can see me and those girls, well, they obviously couldn't."

"Why couldn't they see someone standing right in front of them?" she asked quietly, not really expecting him to be able to explain. "And why do you look so odd? Where did you get that clothing from with that strange picture sewn into it? I have never seen clothes dyed in that colour before and who would sew a complicated pattern like that into something you wear to school? Why aren't you wearing the same clothes as all the other boys?"

Eddie looked down again at his jumper, pulling it out slightly to inspect the logo sewn into the top corner. He had never thought about it before nor wondered how it had been sewn into the jumper.

"Well, I suppose it's my school uniform. Caps and ...er... jackets are not part of our school uniform," he muttered, also wondering why the girl was dressed so strangely.

"Uniform? What's that?" she asked.

"It's what I have to wear to school, of course," he answered. She didn't seem to understand.

"What is your school called? Where is it?" said the girl, in a serious voice.

"St Paul's," answered Eddie, having to think for a moment in order to remember the name of his new school. "And it is in a town called Stoneham Cross. It was only my second day."

Worryingly, his lip started to tremble as he thought of his mother coming to collect him at the end of the day and him not being there. He prided himself on not crying, and especially not in front of girls. He squeezed his eyes shut for a moment to try and collect himself, counting down from ten in a bid to control his breathing as he had been taught.

"Well, this is St Paul's," said the girl in a firm, but not un-friendly, voice. "And it is also in Stoneham Cross, so I think you must be a bit confused. We can't both be in the same school. Maybe you have got lost as it is only your second day? Maybe my friends were just being polite and pretending not to see you as you look so strange?"

Suddenly, Eddie remembered the classroom that he had crawled through so quickly to escape the voices which were walking up the corridor and which threatened to catch him. He wondered if the adults those voices had belonged to would have been able to see him.

He shuddered as he questioned if he had died and was now a ghost; a ghost that only this strange girl could see. Nothing made sense and his head was beginning to pound and he felt lightheaded, almost as if he was going to faint. Urgh, fainting and stuff was only for girls. He couldn't embarrass himself by showing how pathetic he was by toppling over on to the floor. But then, if he was a ghost, how could he faint? He was sure ghosts didn't faint. The thoughts started swirling around in his head, buzzing about like a swarm of bees. He reached his hands up and clasped his head around his ears.

"Why are you doing that?" she said, concerned.

"My head hurts," he had to admit. "I don't feel good."

She stepped over to him, and took him by the arm. He felt her hand strong under his arm and the buzzing intensified as if the bees had been alarmed by an attacking swarm. Through the confusion in his head, he reasoned that if he had been a ghost, surely he wouldn't be able to feel her hand on his arm.

"Let me help you," she said softly, her white pinafore brushing against his knees. "We will have to go into class in a minute. I could ask Miss Hope to help. She is strict but I believe she has a kind heart and could maybe help you find your way back to your own school, wherever that is."

"Miss Hope," whined Eddie. "Who the bloody hell is that?"

She dropped his arm instantly and stepped back, almost stumbling.

"How can you use words like that?" she demanded. "If Miss Hope hears you say that, you will surely be given six strikes."

"Six strikes? What on earth are you on about?"

"Six strikes of the cane, of course," spat the girl, glancing around her and leaning in towards his face so that no one else could hear. "And you would certainly deserve it!"

Eddie's nose was now running and he was struggling to keep the tears out of his eyes. More than ever, he wished he was at home in the electronic glare of his bedroom, his computer and games console keeping him company and promising the comfort of Trickster and *Crash or Dash*. He wished, more than ever, that he was just a normal boy with a normal life, who had never pushed Liam, never been suspended and who had joined in with an everyday football match with his everyday friends at break-time.

The words "cane", "Miss Hope", "strikes" all clanged around in his head, so he pressed his hands tighter and tighter.

In the distance he heard a bell ringing. He dropped his hands slowly. He recognised the sound. It was the same as the bell which was rung at school to announce the end of break time. Exactly the same sound, he was sure.

And, like a flash, he saw the letters September 15th 1898 in front of him just as he had seen them written on the board in the classroom. He saw the girl still there, still watching his every movement.

"What is today's date?" he asked, his voice shaking with a growing realisation.

"Oh," she responded. "Everyone knows it is the fifteenth of September."

"Yes, but what *year*?"

"Eighteen hundred and ninety eight, of course."

CHAPTER 7

"*Eighteen hundred and ninety eight*?" Eddie could hardly get the words out of his mouth.

"Of course, but you must know that! Surely you are not a simpleton?"

"The date today, for me, is the fifteenth of September twenty eighteen. Oh my God...er goodness," he corrected himself quickly, not wanting to annoy her again.

"Twenty eighteen?" she muttered, not understanding. "What sort of a date is that? Twenty and an eighteen?"

"The year two thousand and eighteen."

Her mouth dropped open.

"Are you telling me the truth? No, no, you can't be. This simply can't be right. It is against the laws of nature." She looked shocked and nervous.

"I am telling you," he was nearly shouting now. "I must have travelled back in time. I went into the cupboard in the corridor behind the classroom to see what was in there and when I came out... well, I was here!" He looked at her desperately. He needed to find some proof of where, and when, he was.

Eddie thought back to the classroom with its large blackboard and wooden tables and benches. He remembered the picture of the stern-looking queen, which took pride of place on the wall. He hadn't recognised her at all.

"I saw a picture of a queen on the wall of the classroom," he said, thinking this might help him find out what was going on. "Who is she?"

"Queen Victoria, of course. Everyone knows who *she* is," she said, amazed at his ignorance.

"But our queen is Queen Elizabeth the Second."

"But there has only been one Queen Elizabeth and she lived hundreds of years ago," said the girl, more hesitantly. "You can't be telling the truth."

The bell stopped its insistent ringing and the sound of children running to the classroom forced the girl to drag her eyes away from the sight of Eddie, nose running, eyes watery and with a face full of fear. He could see her trying to make sense of what was going on.

"I don't believe you," she stated firmly.

"What is your name?" asked Eddie, momentarily thinking this was the first time he had ever asked a girl her name. He usually tried to avoid ever speaking to them.

"Charlotte," answered the now-named Charlotte, eyeing him with a frown. "What is yours?"

"Eddie," he answered, thinking that telling this girl his name was another first for him.

"Well, Eddie," said Charlotte, a little crossly, having now decided that what he had said couldn't be true. "I have to go back to my lessons now. I don't know what you are, a spirit, a ghost or a figment of my imagination. There is no possibility that you can have travelled back in time, so you must be something my mind has dreamt up.

"My mother is always telling me I think too much and should have my mind set on more important matters, such as helping in the bakery or with the laundry. You are my punishment for dreaming."

And with that she turned on her heels and walked away to join her afternoon lessons.

Eddie ran after her, the fainting feeling in his legs making it difficult for him to move quickly. As he caught up with her, they turned the corner into the playground and he could see the other children in their drab clothes, white pinafores, boots and caps, trotting towards the school entrance.

As he grabbed her arm, she swung around and glared at him. The sensation of touching her arm made the fizzing in his head instantly worse, but he wanted to prove he was telling the truth and that she needed to believe him.

"I am real," he gasped. She twisted her head away.

"You may be the devil for all I know. Keep away from me, bad spirit," Charlotte snapped back.

"I am NOT a bad spirit. I am a boy from the 21st century. I can prove it to you. Just you wait."

"You are not real, and I will never see you again. Go away."

And with that, Charlotte skipped breathlessly over to her group of friends, who turned to her with smiles. She whispered something to the group and they turned briefly to look in Eddie's direction before turning back to her and shaking their heads.

As Charlotte walked into the classroom entrance, she briefly glanced back at Eddie, standing in full sight in the playground. The girl flicked her head as if to shake the idea of him out of it.

Eddie wanted to prove to her that he did exist and that he was real. He was not a bad spirit, ghost or figment of her imagination but a real, breathing boy.

However, he also was a boy who had to figure out how to return to his own school and time. If he could.

CHAPTER 8

Eddie wondered how long it had been since he stepped into the cupboard. As annoying as his mum was, he still loved her and hated the thought that she would be called up to school because he had disappeared. He questioned how long it would be before the teachers realised he had gone. He had no idea.

His priority now was to get back to his own time and, leaning back against the cool, brick wall, he knew his only option was to go back into the cupboard. If that had been his way in, it must also be the way back out.

Although Charlotte's friends had not been able to see him, Eddie couldn't be certain that he was invisible to everyone except that strange, pale girl who had looked at him so directly and then dismissed him with such cruel words.

How dare she call him a "bad spirit", even though the sight of Liam careering backwards and smacking his arm hard on the play equipment did flash through his head. That had just been a mistake, and he couldn't help it if sometimes he could not control his anger. Was he a "bad spirit" after all? The thought made him feel uncomfortable.

He looked around at the school playground, which was both so familiar and so strange. The school was surrounded by fields and a few brick houses with smoke seeping up into the sky from their chimneys. The small wood, which he remembered from his own school playground, was there, with the tall oak tree standing proudly in the middle. However, all the modern houses, which pressed up against the playground, had gone. There was a feeling of space and openness, which was pleasant, although strange. Less crowded and less busy. Eddie felt his head was busy a lot of the time.

He decided he couldn't return to the corridor the way he had come, through those *Boys* and *Girls* doors leading into the classroom, which would now be full of children. Looking down the wall, towards the trees, he spotted another door at the side of the building. He darted towards this other entrance and stood in front of it, panting slightly. Studying it carefully, he calculated that it would open into the far end of the corridor of coat hooks. If it opened at all.

Gingerly, he turned the knob, wondering how he could actually touch and move things in this world if he was essentially invisible to it. The handle moved and the door opened slightly. Eddie peered through the crack and down the corridor, which ran the length of the classroom he had previously crawled through. The corridor was empty, although he could hear an adult's voice speaking sternly from the classroom and children's voices responding.

He tiptoed down the corridor. The voices grew louder. His legs felt increasingly wobbly and his shaking was getting worse, and he had a strong feeling that he needed to get out of this place. And soon.

There was the doorknob, shining in the gloom. He noticed the smooth metal had no lines or patterns on it. The sandtimer, counting time as the sand dripped through, was missing. He wondered why.

He touched the doorknob, feeling the tingling electric sensation shooting up his arm and almost making him release his grasp. Forcing himself to carry on turning, Eddie kept his eyes peeled on the corridor in case any adult should appear.

The door swung open. He shot inside and slammed the door behind him. Darkness enveloped him like a nightmare as he slumped backwards. He couldn't see anything at all, not even a flickering light indicating a switch or electronic charging point. Breathing heavily, Eddie noticed the trembling and fizzing feelings gradually disappear and he tried to calm himself down. The buzzing in his head subsided and he counted slowly from ten to zero.

Now was the time. He had to be brave and hope. Hope that he was back in his own school, even though he felt a whisper of disappointment that Charlotte had decided he was not real and had called him a "bad spirit". He had told her that he would prove he was real, but the chances of this all happening again must be small.

He grasped the handle tightly and turned it, stepping out into the light.

And there everything was. Just as he had left it. The empty corridor full of bright, colourful bags and coats, and the classroom ahead of him with its cheerful displays, books and red chairs.

"Hey Eddie," said Alfie, as he came into the corridor just moments after Eddie shut the door. "We were wondering where you were. Mrs Jameson is on duty and wants to know why you're not out playing with us!"

"Er, I had to get my snack," said Eddie, turning to fumble in his bag and finding the Kit Kat that they had bought at the Tesco Express. "I'm just coming."

Eddie turned round to look at the door and it stood there silently, hiding what secrets it held in its darkness beyond. He was surprised that no time seemed to have passed at all. It was almost as if he had stepped in and then simply stepped out again. He touched the handle again and nothing happened. No electrical tingling or magnetic pull. It was just an ordinary door. Maybe that was that, he thought. He told himself he must have dreamt it. Had Charlotte been a figment of HIS imagination? Probably, he told himself.

His hand delved into his bag and felt the hard surface of the Kit Kat and he started to pull it out. However, looking towards Alfie standing waiting for him, grinning, he changed his mind and pushed the chocolate bar back into the messy contents of his bag.

"Actually, I will have it at lunchtime," he mumbled to no one in particular. "I'm not that hungry."

And he walked towards the waiting Alfie, telling himself that he was determined to have a go at playing football as, after all, he had promised his mum he would make an effort.

CHAPTER 9

E ddie's mum was on time picking him up that afternoon. She had managed to find a parking space just down the road from the school and they wandered down to the car as she chattered away about her day. Eddie was very quiet.

"What's wrong?" said his mum, turning to him with a worried look on her face. She lifted her hand to peel away a trail of hair that was tickling across her eyes. "Don't tell me you've been naughty again."

"Of course I haven't," said Eddie, immediately cross that she should jump to conclusions. "I am just tired."

Eddie couldn't tell her about what had happened that day as she would never have believed him.

He decided that he didn't believe it himself and that he had probably made the whole thing up when he was shut in the cupboard. At his old school, a lady who was brought in to talk to him about his "anger management" had asked him about his bad dreams, which he had thought was pretty stupid. Maybe this had just been some weird bad dream. A bad day dream. Yes, that was it, he decided firmly.

Eddie was good at shutting things out and this was definitely something that he was going to put a very firm lid on.

It had always just been the two of them, Eddie and his mother, and Eddie was quite happy with that. Although sometimes he did think it would have been nice to have had a dad around like the other kids.

He had never met his dad and his mum never talked about him. If Eddie tried to ask a question about him, his mother would change the subject quickly or look at him sharply with a glance that soon told him to shut up. She told him once that his dad had left a long time ago and that was all he needed to know.

Eddie told himself that at least he didn't get dragged to football practice on a Saturday morning and he didn't have anyone to interfere with his computer time in the evenings. In his previous school, some children told him they were only allowed on the computer for a couple of hours at the weekend. He couldn't imagine a life like that. It would be terrible. The only thing he ever had to look forward to were his evenings spent tapping away on the keyboard or mastering the next level of which ever game was his latest obsession.

Suddenly, Eddie remembered the football game he had half-heartedly joined in with at school that day. He begrudgingly admitted to himself that it wasn't as bad as he thought it might be. He had even kicked the ball a couple of times.

Tea was fish fingers and chips. Eddie and his mother sat in front of the TV with trays balanced on their laps, watching the latest episode of Emmerdale.

As the lights flickered across his cooling chips, Eddie's mind wandered back to Charlotte's pale face and her cross words as she wandered off with her friends. How cool was that, he thought, being able to create all that in his own head?

After tea, Eddie's mum quickly washed up so that she was ready for EastEnders and he was ready to scamper up into his bedroom.

He shut the door firmly behind him and pottered over to his computer, turning it on and watching the machine wake up and stir into action. His mother had bought him the computer as a Christmas present a couple of years ago. It was second-hand, as they didn't have much money, but she often said it was "money well spent" as Eddie spent so much time on it.

Trickster was on good form this evening, his site showing his latest funny stunt which involved standing on a pavement dressed in a luminous workman's high-vis jacket and telling people to walk around an invisible hole in the pavement.

Every single person carefully walked around it just because Trickster told them to and because he was wearing a silly jacket. Eddie laughed out loud. People were so stupid, they just did what they were told, like silly sheep. He wasn't like that, he decided. He would never walk around a hole that wasn't there just because someone told him to. In fact, he didn't really like anyone telling him to do anything. It made him, well... angry. Why did he have to go to school, he wondered? All day long people just told him to do things he didn't want to do.

The light outside started to dim and the electronic flare from the computer became more insistent, lighting up Eddie's face as he stared into it.

He finally clicked off Youtube and decided to have another go at getting to Level 5 on *Crash or Dash*. He hesitated a moment and thought maybe there was a tip online that could help him. He clicked on to Google.

But instead of typing in a question about how to beat the dare-devil Ferrari driver and reach the next level, he found himself typing something completely different. *1898*. He stared at the numbers he had created in the Google search engine. Then he clicked Return.

The search results showed a load of Wikipedia results that he didn't understand and which looked really boring, so he added the words *kids* and *school*. Pressed return again.

When the screen whirled into a list of suggestions, he quickly scanned down to one that looked interesting. It was a BBC page that announced it was about "Victorian children at school". He bit his thumb nervously. *Victorian*? He was sure Charlotte said something about the queen being called Victoria.

He clicked on the page link and his eyes widened as he flicked through the photos. The children in the photos were dressed just like the kids he had seen in his bad day dream. Long dresses covered by white aprons, boys in caps and jackets.

He sat, staring at the screen for a while, confused.

In a flash, he jumped up and went out of his room and scuttled down the stairs. He walked hesitantly into the sitting room, where his mother was lying with her feet up on the sofa, now watching an episode of DIY SOS, a glass of wine in her hand.

"Mum," he asked, and she turned her head towards him, her eyes still watching the television.

"Yes, baby," she answered, still engrossed with the sight of workmen scrambling over each other in a half-knocked down house.

"Have you ever heard of a queen called Victoria?"

"Why?" she said, absent-mindedly.

Eddie hesitated, not wanting to tell the whole truth: "Oh, we have to do a project on her."

"Oh yes, everyone has heard of Queen Victoria," she said, now glued to the presenter complaining, once again, that rain was threatening to ruin the house repair project.

"When was she queen?"

"Oh goodness, I don't know. Maybe a hundred years ago. She was married to someone called Prince Albert and he died and she was really sad so she wore black all the time – for years and years. She was a bit of a miserable old so and so, I think."

"Was she queen in 1898?" Eddie almost hoped she would tell him she wasn't, and then he would know the whole thing was just a load of old rubbish.

"Er, yes, probably, babes. Do you mind if I watch this? I'm really exhausted and need to chill out. I bet the rain doesn't ruin it all. They say that every week and they always finish it on time."

She turned her head back to her TV programme and sipped at her wine.

"I am really pleased you are doing your project," she added. "Go and carry on with it while I watch this."

Eddie walked slowly back upstairs.

Somehow Trickster and *Crash or Dash* had lost their glow. He had a strange feeling that it might not have been a bad dream at all.

And, although he was nervous and scared, he knew there was only one way to find out.

CHAPTER 10

I t was at lunchtime the following day that disaster struck. Eddie had had an OK morning, managing to look interested enough in "how to punctuate dialogue" in English and "addition using the compact method" in maths, to avoid his teacher taking much notice of him.

He made some effort to put in the correct punctuation and, as usual, the calculations in maths came easily to him without much trying. He even found he almost enjoyed the satisfaction of coming up with the correct answers.

He remembered Mrs Jameson's comments about his work being messy, and made some effort to make it neater. Just to keep her off his back, Eddie told himself.

However, Ethan, with the freckles and toothy grin, was a different story.

He happily told Eddie, as they attempted their maths calculations, that he was "dyslexic", as if it was something special and exciting. He also added, for extra drama, that he was asthmatic and had to have an inhaler which he needed to bring with him whenever he did PE. Just in case. It was almost as if he enjoyed his various problems and thought that Eddie would be impressed. Eddie wasn't.

Eddie knew what asthma was as several children in his previous school had claimed they suffered from it. They were always grabbing their silly inhalers when they went out to PE or on a school trip. Eddie had found them all annoying. However, he had never come across "dyslexic" before.

"So, what does dyslexic mean then?" he asked Ethan, slightly cross with himself that he had taken the bait and entered into some sort of conversation.

The other boy explained with a big, toothy grin that it meant his letters got jumbled up and he sometimes didn't understand instructions.

Eddie noticed it also meant that Mrs Jameson spent a lot of time looking at his work, checking he knew what the instructions were and that he knew what to do. Eddie was happy to be left to his own devices and put in just enough effort to hopefully slip under the teacher's radar. He felt very superior to Ethan, and almost pitied the boy for the amount of attention the teachers gave him.

At lunchtime, Alfie tried again to get Eddie to come and play football with them. Eddie knew it was just because Mrs Jameson had told him to look after the new boy and it was humiliating. They all needed to realise he liked to be left alone and didn't like games like football. Even though, he did have to admit, it had been almost fun the other break when he had joined in for a bit.

However, Eddie now had other things on his mind, as he wanted to have another try at going into the cupboard and seeing if he could enter that other, strange world and find Charlotte. He needed to prove to her that he was not a "bad spirit". He thought the lunchbreak might offer a good opportunity and being forced to play football would ruin his plans.

However, Alfie couldn't seem to take "no" for an answer and made the mistake of going on and on at him. Eddie could feel himself begin to get angry. He clenched his fists and dug his nails into the palms of his hands. The two boys stood facing eachother at the end of the corridor, by the toilets.

"Oh come on," said Alfie. "You enjoyed it the other day, didn't you? You can't spend the rest of your time at this school playing with no one else."

"I have TOLD you," growled Eddie, glaring at Alfie, his voice low and menacing. "I don't want to play your stupid games. Just leave me alone."

It was at this moment that Ethan came shooting out of the boys' toilets, tucking his shirt into his trousers. He had his usual friendly grin on his face, but was momentarily looking down at his shirt, rather than where he was going.

Ethan barged headlong into Eddie, who instinctively, without thinking, lifted his hands up to push him away. Hard.

Ethan's eyes shot up in shock as he toppled backwards, tripping on a bag strewn in the walkway. It all happened in slow motion. He seemed to fly back, his head cracking on one of the coat hooks. Ethan's eyes rolled back as he gently, horrifyingly, slumped to the floor. Blood trickled down the side of his face.

"Oh my God!" shouted Alfie. "He's dead!"

Eddie stared, openmouthed, at the boy slumped on the floor in front of him. What had he done? He needed to run, to escape, to get away from the nightmare that was happening all over again.

All hell broke loose around Ethan, who was now sitting up, rubbing his head and looking around him in confusion.

Teachers gathered around, pushing the children, who had crowded around for a good look, out of the way and taking control of the situation.

Eddie panicked. He knew he had to escape and grabbed his chance. He stepped quietly back towards the door and felt behind him for the handle. He could feel the grooves of the sandtimer and the electricity shooting up his arm. Holding his breath against the strange buzzing in his hand, he managed to twist the knob, open the door behind him and slip in. The teachers and children, who were all gathered around Ethan on the floor, barely registered his existence.

He shut the door gently and crossed his fingers, hoping that he would end up anywhere except in his own school and in his own life. He couldn't get the sight of Ethan toppling backwards, his head making that horrible cracking sound, out of his mind. That had not been part of his plan at all.

The darkness in the cupboard was like a blanket, holding him tight away from the madness outside. What was his mother going to say? Was he going to be suspended again?

When he touched the door handle again, he felt the magnetic electricity flicker up his arm. Slowly, hesitantly, he pushed the door and peered out of the crack.

He saw tiles on the floor and the dust sweeping up into the high ceiling and knew that he had escaped the nightmare of the present and had returned to this strange place in the past. He breathed a heavy sigh of relief.

Eddie tiptoed out into the corridor.

The distant sound of children playing was familiar from last time and he expected he knew what those children would look like – very different to his own school.

He remembered that Charlotte seemed to be the only person who could see him and he had no idea how that could be possible. How could he open doors or even stand on the floor if he didn't actually exist for anyone in this world, except Charlotte. Maybe he was now in another, different, time and she wouldn't even be here.

A part of him felt sad at that thought, as he didn't like the thought that she believed he was some sort of devil.

The thought of Ethan's face, with the trickle of blood, flashed before him. Well, maybe he was just that. A devil and bad spirit. Maybe that was how he could travel between two different times. How awful, to know that you are a bad spirit. Eddie stifled a sob.

He slumped down to the floor, his hands resting between his knees and dangling sadly. His head was bowed and a tear ran down his face. Wiping it away with his sleeve, he looked around him, pushing his long, curly hair away from his eyes.

Voices again. Coming down the corridor. He wondered if he should brave it and stay where he was, just to see if they were able to see him or not.

However, as the voices got closer, his nerve failed him and he ran to the end of the corridor, to the door that he had used last time to come in from the playground.

He opened it and stepped out, looking around him. He crept down the edge of the wall and peered around the corner. Once again, children filled the playground, playing with unusual toys and wearing those strange, drab, boring clothes. But they were all still children, with the same laughs, giggles, shouts and cries that he heard on the playground at his own school.

He wondered where the girl was. Charlotte. He knew he wanted to see her and talk to her, as she seemed to be his only human connection to this peculiar place. He noticed her sitting on a bench at the other end of the school. Her friends were all playing around her, occasionally going over and sitting next to her, smiling and chatting.

She looked, if anything, paler and thinner than last time. Her hand went to her mouth every few minutes as she coughed and clasped her chest.

Eddie was now standing in full sight of the children running around. None of them took any notice of him at all. It was as if he didn't exist, but strangely they never actually came close to touching him. When he moved towards them, they were driven away by an invisible force and any hoop or ball which came near, swerved delicately around him as if by magic.

He remembered that when Charlotte had touched him, he had felt that buzzing sensation. There was clearly something that made him real to her and her to him.

He strode confidently now through the groups of playing children. No child even glanced in his direction.

Until he reached Charlotte.

The instant he stood before her, her brown eyes looked up and met his.

He could see her briefly wondering whether to acknowledge that he was there and admit she could see him.

Or pretend she couldn't see the "bad spirit" and carry on with her life, never knowing who he was and where he had come from.

CHAPTER 11

When she spoke, he knew which side of the argument had won.

"So, you are here again," she whispered.

One of Charlotte's friends stopped midway through hopping to collect a stone she had thrown on to a series of chalk squares drawn on the playground. The girl glanced over in Charlotte's direction.

"Sorry, Charlotte," she said. "Did you say something?"

"No, Emily," answered Charlotte, all the time staring at Eddie. "I was just thinking about the poem we have to recite this afternoon. Seeing if I could remember it."

"Oh goodness," Emily laughed. "You are so stuffy. I expect you will want to get full marks again!"

She skipped off after the stones she had thrown and left Charlotte and Eddie alone.

The girl made a little movement with her hand to indicate they should go over to the trees at the other end of the school and looked around her to question whether anyone else had seen Eddie or if he was truly invisible to everyone – except her.

"I am just going to sit under the trees for a moment," she said to her friends.

They nodded and carried on with their games without looking back.

Eddie trotted after her as she made her way over to the oak tree. She went to the back of its trunk and sat down on the ground, presumably so that no one could see her talking to thin air. Eddie sat down next to her. She coughed again and he heard a rattle deep inside her chest, as she held a handkerchief to her mouth. Eddie noticed she had the letters CS sewn into one corner of the white material.

"How long is it since I was last here?" he asked.

"It was about a week ago," she said. "I must admit I have been looking out for you ever since."

Maybe she no longer believed he was a "bad spirit" then.

"What happened after I left you?" she asked, looking awkward. Eddie wondered if she was embarrassed about the nasty comments she had made before she ran off.

"Well, I went back through the cupboard and found myself back in my school," answered Eddie. " It was as if I had never been away. I came out of it just seconds after I went in." He started kicking his foot at the bark on the ground.

"So, who are you?" she asked.

"Why should I tell you, if you don't believe me?" said Eddie. "You said I was a bad spirit."

"I have thought about what I said," said the girl, fiddling with the edge of her white apron and looking down at the ground. "I didn't know what to think. You looked so different and strange, and talked of a new queen and a new time in the future. I suppose I was a little scared by you. I am sorry if I wasn't very kind. I didn't think I would ever see you again, yet here you are."

She turned and looked at him with her brown eyes, and her pale skin shimmered in the dappled light from the tree above them, sheltering them with its age-old branches.

"Please explain to me who you are," she said simply.

And so Eddie told her who he was and where he came from. About how he lived in the future, about his mother, moving to Stoneham Cross because of his "trouble" at his previous school, about how he didn't like football or have any friends, and how he had just hurt a boy at his school. He had never spoken to anyone like this in his life before.

Charlotte studied the ground silently, taking in everything

that he said and not commenting or showing what she thought in any way. After he finished, she coughed a little again and held her handkerchief thoughtfully to her mouth.

"This world you live in is very strange," she said. "Are you saying you live one hundred and twenty years in the future? Is this the world in one hundred and twenty years' time?"

"I suppose it must be," he answered.

"So what will your punishment be for what you did to this other boy?" asked Charlotte.

"I suppose I will have to go to see the headteacher," mumbled Eddie. "And then mum will be called up to school. I might have to stay in at lunchtime or maybe even get suspended."

"Suspended?" her eyes flew open in shock. "Suspended from what? Do you really mean they would hang you up somewhere? How long for?" She grasped his hand in concern. A buzzing feeling shot up his arm.

"What? I don't know what you are talking about. I mean suspended as in having to stay at home for a day."

She dropped his hand like a stone. He realised she had taken "suspended" as meaning "hung" from something. Urgh, how horrible.

"So, your punishment for hurting this boy is a talk, and then you are sent home?" she said. "How many strikes would you get?"

"Strikes?"
"Strikes of the cane?"

Eddie remembered reading on the BBC website that Victorian children were hit with a stick if they were naughty – he remembered it was called a "cane" and that Charlotte had mentioned it the last time they had met.

"We don't have canes in our school," said Eddie. She looked surprised.

"So you don't have the cane, but you have talks with the headteacher and are sent home for the day. How very strange," said the pale girl, as she nibbled at her fingers. "Maybe your mother or father would cane you?"

"Hardly," said Eddie. "I don't have a dad and my mum is just annoyed that I interrupt her social life when I have to stay at home from school. She knows I hate school."

Charlotte sat and thought about everything she had heard for a few moments. It was difficult to take it all in and Eddie watched her try to understand. He also had so many questions to ask, but he had a sense that this moment was for him to explain to her, and Charlotte's chance to talk about her life would come later.

He thought about how good she was to talk to, how she listened carefully and had a stillness and wisdom about her that he had not come across before. Eddie realised that he actually enjoyed talking to her and being with her – a feeling he didn't have very often.

"I can't believe that," Charlotte said quietly.

"What?"

"That you hate school. Education is the most important thing in my life," said the girl decidedly. "It is the most precious thing in the world."

"What? Boring lessons and teachers who boss you around all day long? I hate it."

Charlotte spun around to face him.

"My parents work as bakers in the village," she said, bitterly. "They work most of the night and well into the day. They give me a good life but they cannot give me what I want. I want to work hard and be somebody in the world. I have a good brain, but they think that because I am a girl, I should be working at home and thinking about having a husband and a home."

"But you are only about ten years old!" Eddie said, shocked.

"This school only teaches us until we are ten and then we have to leave. Next year, I will have to go and help my parents in the bakery."

"Well, that doesn't sound too bad," answered Eddie. "A nice little job with some pocket money and no teachers bossing you around all day."

She looked at him with her large, brown eyes.

"When that time comes, when I have to give up school, learning, education and all the promises of the future, my life is finished. My greatest dream would be to study until I know everything I can possibly know."

"Well you should visit my time with me, then," said Eddie. "Because we have school until we are eighteen."

"Just for boys, I expect," said Charlotte, sadly.

"Oh no, both boys and girls."

"Well, I wish I lived one hundred and twenty years in the future then."

She looked at the ground, coughing gently in that strange, quiet way. She laid her hand on her chest and caught her breath.

"What is it like, then?" asked the girl. "What is it like in your future?"

Eddie hardly knew where to start. He looked around him at the trees, the fields, the open skies with no aeroplane trails weaving their white paths across the blue. There was no noise, except the laughing sounds of children and the birds singing in the trees above. No cars. No lorries. No bits of plastic rubbish captured in the corner of the playground fence.

"Well, of course we have computers," he answered, thinking of what he imagined to be the biggest, and best, difference between her time and his.

"Computers? What are they?"

"They are like boxes of electronics that hold huge amounts of information," he lamely tried to explain. "You sort of turn them on and you can go anywhere in the world and find out anything you want."

"Electronics? I wonder what that means," she continued. "How do you work this box? Is it magic? Would the vicar approve – he doesn't like magic?"

"I dunno," muttered Eddie. "I have never met our vicar. I don't know if we even have one."

"Is the future so godless, then? I go to church every Sunday with my whole family. Most of the people in the village do."

"At my old school, we went at Christmas," said Eddie.

"So this box is a sort of magic electronic that gives you all the information you want. Goodness, how fantastic that would be. I could read books on this box, I could find out about new lands and places, I could help cure people who are ill."

"Oh no, I don't bother with any of that," Eddie laughed, without thinking. "I play games on it. Every evening. That is my favourite thing in the world."

"You play games?" she echoed. "You have the magic box of all the knowledge in the world and you play games. What sort of games?"

Eddie started to shift uncomfortably on the hard ground. He suddenly had a suspicion she might not find his games quite as amazing as he did.

"Er, I, well, I sort of race cars and try and crash into people," he said awkwardly.

"Cars?"

"Like carts but instead of being pulled by horses, you drive them with motors – but they go really, really fast."

"I think my father mentioned something about carts on wheels that have motors to drive them. They are a new invention," whispered Charlotte, clearly thinking back to a conversation with her father.

The game now sounded a little bit silly.

"So your game," she continued simply. "Do your friends all join in with this? Is that why you do it?"

"No," he said sullenly. "I play on my own. That is how I like it."

She shook her head silently. The future was clearly not looking so great in her eyes.

"I don't like being alone. I like to be with my friends and my family. People are very precious. After all, they are sometimes here for so short a time."

He sat silently, waiting for her to continue. Charlotte stared sadly into the distance.

"Two of my sisters died before they reached two years old. One died of whooping cough, the other of scarlet fever. Maybe your magic box could have helped them."

"Yes, maybe it could," agreed Eddie, having no idea at all what whooping cough and scarlet fever were. He decided, for the first time in his life, that maybe computers weren't such a great topic of conversation.

The bell started ringing across the playground, signalling that it was time to go back into lessons. Charlotte got up reluctantly.

"I would love to know more about your time, but I have to go back to class."

Suddenly, Eddie had a brainwave.

"Why don't you come back with me now? I bet you are invisible in my time just as I am in yours!"

Charlotte considered what he was saying, fiddling gently with the edge of the white handkerchief she was holding in her hand. She was clearly interested. Eddie could see the idea of a future with education for boys and girls appealed to her and he found that a bit strange. However, it would be fun to show her how different it was in his time. The sight of Ethan lying crumpled on the floor flashed before him, reminding him that things might not be so great for him when he returned to the present day. But the thought of Charlotte being there to see his modern world was too tempting to stop him trying to persuade her. If he told her, it might put her off trying.

"If I get caught, the consequences would be greater than they would be for you," she said solemnly. "I would definitely get the cane, that's for certain."

"But if it worked, it would be amazing," said Eddie, solemnly, wondering himself what punishment awaited him once they discovered it was he who had pushed Ethan. At least it wouldn't be the cane.

He watched her think carefully, weighing up whether the risk was worth it. She looked suspiciously at him, wondering if she could trust him. The bell kept clanging in the distance, hurrying her decision.

"All right then," she decided. "Let's try it. I have to see this world in the future, if what you say is really true. But if it fails, I will be in very big trouble."

The pair of children, one with a bright red jumper and so invisible, the other with a pale white smock and entirely visible to everyone, half ran, half walked across the playground. Eddie held Charlotte's hand to show her which door he had gone through. He felt the electricity of her touch buzzing through his arm. There was something very different about her. She had an energy, a determination that set her apart from anyone he had ever met.

Eddie opened the door, which led from the side of the school into the corridor. The dust danced in the beams of light that shone through the windows. The cupboard door stood silently in the middle. They made a dash for it, running swiftly down the tiles, grabbing the handle and throwing themselves inside. They clamped the door shut behind them. Their breathing echoed around in the darkness and they could feel the tension and fear of the other person.

After a minute, when their breathing had slowed, Eddie whispered: "Shall we do it?"

"Yes," said Charlotte, nervously.

She grasped the handle and turned to face the door. Confident in the knowledge that she would be invisible to everyone except Eddie in this new world of the future, she opened it quickly and stepped out, with Eddie close behind her.

"Charlotte Simmonds! WHAT ARE YOU DOING?" a fierce voice echoed down the corridor.

Charlotte glanced back at Eddie in terror. He saw her eyes wide with alarm and her mouth open in shock. He tried to grasp her hand, but she pushed him away and the handkerchief she had been holding came away in his grasp.

He stepped back into the cupboard, seeing the tiles beneath her feet and the wooden ceiling soaring above. He was still holding her handkerchief tightly in his grip.

She pushed the door shut behind her, shutting him inside and leaving her on the outside.

The angry, shouting voice was silenced in an instant. All

Eddie could hear was the pounding of his heart.

CHAPTER 12

The darkness boomed and swirled around him as he tried to find some light in the cupboard. His breathing was fast and ragged.

So, Charlotte had stepped right back into her own time and not his future.

Eddie was suddenly very worried for her, imagining her being dragged into the headteacher's office and goodness know what happening to her. He felt a coward, hiding in the cupboard and not being able to help her in any way. His chest heaved and his eyes darted about, unable to make out any shape or object in the dark room.

Eddie decided he did not want to be a coward and that he had to help his new friend. He tried to calm himself for a moment, thinking about what he could possibly do in a world where no one saw him. Could he grab a piece of chalk and write a message on the board? That might just scare everyone and maybe make them think Charlotte was some sort of witch or something.

He remembered seeing a film (he thought it might have been one of the 15-rated films his mum sometimes let him watch with her) about witches where they were hunted down and burnt at the stake. He never admitted it, but that film had given him nightmares for months. His mum had thought the film was funny.

No, that wasn't a good idea. He tried to think calmly. He banged his hand on his head a little to try and shake a brainwave into it, but the thoughts just rattled and buzzed around point-lessly.

Perhaps the best thing to do would be to just go back and take things as he found them. You never know, he thought to him-self, she might have been telling tales and exaggerating things. Somehow, that didn't seem possible... not with Charlotte any-way. She didn't seem the sort of person to exaggerate.

As he stood in the darkness trying to make sense of what had just happened, he felt the electricity shoot up and down his arms. The strange sensation made him feel quite dizzy and he put his hand on the wall to steady himself. He was still holding the handkerchief tightly between his fingers and he could feel the swarm of energy travel down his arm and circle around his hand. The handkerchief started to vibrate and shake in his fin-gers but he could see nothing in the deep darkness.

Then, in a second of buzzing fury, the handkerchief suddenly bulged in his hand and collapsed in a heap of dust. The tiny par-ticles ran through his fingers onto the floor of the cupboard. It was completely gone.

Eddie had a horrible feeling he was now beyond being able to help Charlotte and that the moment for action had passed. He gulped down a big mouthful of air and turned the handle as Charlotte had done just seconds before. This time, however, he just opened it a tiny crack. The light streamed through and Eddie had a moment to scan around the cupboard and see it was full of old boxes and bits of wood. Almost as if it had been for-gotten for years.

He looked back through the crack and his face fell. A bright collection of coats, polystyrene rain-stained tiles and bags scat-tered around. He was back in his own time and he had left Char-lotte to her uncertain fate on her own. And he now had to face his own.

It was as if time had stood still.

Ethan was sitting rubbing his head. Alfie was looking on, con-cerned. Mrs Jameson and the other adults were shooing the chil-dren outside, and Mr Evans was trotting towards them down the corridor, holding his tie to stop it flapping over his shoulder.

"What happened here?" asked Mr Evans, bending down to check the cut on Ethan's cheek. Eddie held his breath, knowing what was coming next.

"Well," said Ethan, uncertainly. "I was coming out of the toilets and I must have been looking down at my shoes or something cos the next thing I knew, I bumped into someone and then tripped over. I think I must have hit my head. Cor, it really hurts." He lifted his hand up to touch the cut on the side of his head.

"Were you here, Alfie?" asked Mr Evans. "Did you see what happened?"

Alfie nodded. Eddie held his breath.

"I was talking to Eddie," he said, nodding in the direction of the other boy, now standing next to the cupboard door.

Eddie looked down at his shoes and clenched and unclenched his fists. He felt the usual feeling of fury start to seep through his skin as he immediately started to make excuses for what he had done. But something held him back. An understanding that, in some way, he might be to blame and maybe this time he should be brave and admit what he had done.

"And," continued Alfie. "Well, Ethan came charging out of the toilets and wasn't looking where he was going. Eddie put his hands up quickly like this," Alfie demonstrated helpfully. "Then Ethan just ran straight into him. He fell back and I think he tripped on something and then he hit his head. I thought he was dead!"

Eddie looked down the corridor at the group surrounding Ethan in confusion. Why weren't they blaming him? Why weren't they dragging him down to the headteacher's office for a telling off and a phone call to his mum? He had caused Ethan to fall over and he, for the first time in his life, was prepared to pay the consequences.

"Er, Mr Evans," said Eddie. Mr Evans looked up from inspecting Ethan's head and stared straight at Eddie.

"Yes, Eddie. Have you something to say?"

"Well, I think it must have been my fault," stuttered Eddie. "I think I must have pushed him before he fell."

No one in the world could have any idea what it took for Eddie to utter that admission. To suddenly feel in any way responsible for something that had happened, and not blame it on someone else.

Eddie himself was surprised by his own words, and wondered where they had come from. The sight of Charlotte, stepping out of the cupboard to face the fury of her teacher, fleetingly flashed before Eddie's eyes. He had tried to be brave to save her then. He was trying to be brave again now.

"Hmmn," considered Mr Evans. "From what Alfie and Ethan say, I think it must have been more of an accident than something you did on purpose. You all need to look where you are going.

"Come on, Ethan. We need to get you into the office, fill out an accident report, and call your parents. They probably need to get you checked out., although you seem to be all in working order!"

Ethan stood up shakily and Mr Evans and Mrs Jameson led him down the corridor towards the office, leaving Alfie and Eddie alone, all of the onlookers having been sent outside.

Eddie was nervous about what Alfie was going to say next and started thinking about possible ways to respond to the blame Alfie was going to heap on him. Perhaps he had a reason for saying that it was an accident and wanted Eddie to pay him back for it. Lots of unpleasant possibilities swirled in his head.

"So, are you coming?" said Alfie, surprisingly.

"Where?"

"Out to play football?" answered Alfie, a little irritated. "This is the last time I am going to ask you. I am fed up with asking again and again – even if Mrs Jameson keeps on at me about you being on your own. That's your problem from now on."

"I am coming," said Eddie, causing Alfie to look at him in astonishment.

"Really?"

"Yes, really," said the new boy, surprising himself. "Let's go and play football. Mr Evans seemed to think Ethan will be OK."

Alfie smiled broadly at him and jogged off down the corridor to find what football drama was being staged today on the playground and Eddie stood for a few moments on his own in the corridor.

He briefly looked at the door and wondered what was happening back in Charlotte's time. He glanced at the swirls and stars on the door, the sandtimer which was carved into the metal. There had been no pattern on the handle of the door in Charlotte's school. That was strange, he thought.

And as he studied it for a few moments, he saw that the sand in the top part of the timer was no longer full. Some had trickled from the top into the bottom, he was certain. Or maybe it was just a trick of the light.

That evening, Eddie crept up to his room after his TV dinner of pizza and ice cream was finished. As Coronation Street whined into action with its tell-tale signature tune, Eddie turned on his computer. He didn't even bother to touch his console as his mind was definitely on other things. He couldn't help but remember Charlotte's scornful reaction to his interest in *Crash or Dash*.

As the white glare swept around the room, Eddie typed in a Google search. **Punishment in Victorian Schools.** Several possibilities came up and Eddie clicked on the one that appeared to give a simple, straightforward answer.

Teachers often beat pupils using a cane. Canes were mostly made out of birch wood. Boys were usually caned on their backsides and girls were either beaten on their bare legs or across their hands. A pupil could receive a caning for a whole range of different reasons, including: rudeness, leaving a room without permission, laziness, not telling the truth and playing truant (missing school)

His blood ran cold.

Charlotte had told him the truth, as he had suspected. What horrible thing was going to happen to her once the teacher found her stepping out of a forbidden cupboard? And why had she not been able to come into his world, when he could so easily travel back to hers?

Eddie sat with his head in his hands, thinking and thinking. He knew that when he stepped in and out of the cupboard, no time had passed, yet a whole week had passed for Charlotte in her time. Maybe this meant it was impossible for them to both travel together. He thought about the handkerchief crumbling to dust in his fingers.

Did the sandtimer have something to do with it? His mind wandered back to an RE lesson on symbols at his old school. The teacher had explained symbols were pictures which represented another, deeper meaning, he was sure. Maybe the sandtimer on the handle was some sort of symbol.

Remembering Charlotte's excitement that his "magic box" could unlock all sorts of secrets, Eddie did a Google search on "sandtimer". The search revealed that it was called an "hourglass" in ancient times. He searched "hourglass symbol", his hands trembling a little at what he might find. All sorts of weird results leapt up, most of which he couldn't understand. Wikipedia helped a little:

Unlike most other methods of measuring time, the hourglass represents the present as being between the past and the future, and this has made it a symbol of time itself

The words were complicated and confusing. Eddie read and re-read them and gathered that a sandtimer, or hourglass, was a symbol of time and the past and the future. A "symbol of time itself". It made his head hurt, none of it made sense at all. Had the grains of sand on the door handle really started to trickle through the timer? And if they had, what did that mean?

For once in his life, Eddie cared about something beyond

himself. He was concerned and worried about his new friend. Today he had tried to go back and help her, but he had been too late. He also guessed the fact her handkerchief had turned to dust in his hand meant that it was impossible for anything in her time to travel back to his.

But then he thought about the breaktime, which had followed Charlotte's attempt to come back with him. The boy with no friends had been distracted from Charlotte's unknown fate by a whole game of football with the boys (and one girl) in his class. Well, he thought, that was a first.

Life was turning out to be full of surprises – some good and some bad.

CHAPTER 13

The next day, Eddie found himself actually looking forward to going to school. He was up early and pestered his mother to make sure she delivered him to St Paul's on time. For once, there was cereal in the cupboard, milk in the fridge, and they set off in plenty of time.

Ethan turned up with a huge plaster stamped on the side of his head, where he had hit the coat hook. He was treated like a celebrity by the other children in the class, who all gathered around to admire his war wound. He was happy to tell everyone about how he had spent several hours in A&E the previous afternoon, but skimmed quickly over the doctors telling him that it was "just a little cut" and that he would be fine to return to school the next day.

He didn't appear to blame Eddie for what had happened, believing that it had all been an accident and that his classmate hadn't done it on purpose.

Eddie was still not sure he hadn't meant to push Ethan over, but he found himself part of the crowd that listened in admiration to Ethan's lively re-telling of his dash to the emergency room. Eddie didn't even find the attention that Ethan was getting particularly annoying.

At break time, Ethan wasn't allowed to join in the football game and had to sit on the sidelines watching forlornly. He managed to join in with many shouted words of advice, which made Eddie, who had joined in the game without Alfie having to encourage him, actually laugh a few times.

After break it was maths. Mrs Jameson told the class they would be doing some work on times tables and Eddie stifled a yawn and allowed his mind to wander back to Charlotte and think about how he was going to try and go back at lunchtime and see what had happened to her.

"So, what about it, Eddie?" the teacher said suddenly, jerking Eddie out of his plans and schemes.

"Sorry? What?" answered Eddie, looking up through his fringe from where he was slumped on his seat.

"Taking part in the times tables challenge?" said Mrs Jameson, patiently, knowing that her pupil had not listened to a word she said.

"What's that?" he muttered.

The other children looked warily at the teacher, expecting her to tell Eddie off for being impolite. However, she just smiled and explained the challenge was a chance for one of the pupils to compete against the teacher. A competition in front of the whole class... and that none of the pupils had beaten her so far this term.

"Nah," he said, his rudeness making the other children gasp a little.

"Come on. You might even win!" laughed the teacher.

The other children looked at him and started saying "Go on, Eddie" and hammering on the tables. He felt himself start to get hot, and little pulses of anger started to simmer through him. Why should he be bothered with it, he thought? He would probably lose anyway and that would be embarrassing. Glaring around at the other children, he saw Ethan sitting across the table cheering him on with a smile and giving him two thumbs-ups with his hands. He thought about how Ethan had looked yesterday, lying on the floor, blood trickling down his freckled face.

He felt cornered. Pushing his chair back with a sigh, Eddie tried to hide his eyes behind his long hair and slouched forwards unenthusiastically to stand next to his teacher at the front of the class. Alfie volunteered to do the scorekeeping on the board. It was to be the best out of five questions. Whoever was first with the correct answer won the point.

"As you weren't able to play football today, you can be the question master, Ethan," said Mrs Jameson. Ethan bounced to the front of the room, his red hair glinting in the sunshine streaming through the window.

The class was hushed. Eddie told himself he didn't care, despite being aware that his hands were clammy and his face hot.

"Four times six," said Ethan quickly, taking Eddie unawares.

"Twenty four," answered the teacher without hesitation, before Eddie even had a chance to think about the answer. He reminded himself that this was all really stupid and he wasn't bothered at all.

"Seven times three." Again Eddie hadn't even opened his mouth before the teacher gave the correct answer. She looked at Eddie and grinned.

"Two-nil!"

She seems pleased with herself, thought Eddie with annoyance. He knew he was good at maths. Maybe he could win, he thought. He found himself starting to focus and concentrate.

"Eight times nine," chirped Ethan.

"Seventy two."

Eddie realised that he had answered almost automatically, before his teacher had uttered a sound.

"Ooh, two-one!" said Mrs Jameson, not at all concerned that she had lost the point.

"Question four," said Ethan, enjoying the limelight. "Four times twelve."

The correct answer shot from Eddie just a fraction before Mrs Jameson managed to answer.

"Two-all," said Alfie, officiously writing the scores on the whiteboard. "Sudden death question."

Eddie glanced around the classroom. Everyone was holding their breath as they knew their teacher would give it her best. She never let anyone win easily.

"Er," hesitated Ethan. "Let's think of a difficult one. Eleven times twelve."

Eddie's mind raced. Ten times twelve is one hundred and twenty, add another twelve to make ...

He heard himself shout: "One hundred and thirty two!"

The class erupted into an explosion of cheering as Eddie realised that he had beaten the teacher. He felt himself stand up straight and swept his fringe back from his face. Looking up at his teacher, standing next to him, he couldn't help grinning.

She bent down slightly towards him and whispered: "Well done, Eddie. I knew you could do it."

He felt a little bit pleased with himself.

CHAPTER 14

Although he couldn't help feeling proud of his success in the times tables challenge, Eddie couldn't stop thinking about Charlotte and wondering what had happened to her.

When the class was dismissed for lunch, he told Alfie and Ethan that he needed to ask their teacher something and he would meet them on the playground. They went off happily, although Ethan was still annoyed at not being able to join in the lunchtime football game. He disappeared down the corridor, muttering: "I am playing tomorrow, I don't care what anyone says."

Eddie fiddled with his bag until the corridor was quiet. He moved over to the door and stared at it for a moment, looking carefully at the hourglass and noticing it was exactly the same as the last time he had studied it. The sand had trickled part way into the bottom chamber, but maybe it had always been like that. He wasn't sure.

He felt no pull from the door, no electricity or magnetic charge. Stretching his hand out, he touched the metal handle and nothing happened.

Through the window behind him in the classroom, Mrs Jameson was busily sorting out books and changing the presentation on the interactive whiteboard, ready for the afternoon lessons. Eddie hoped she couldn't see him.

He grasped the handle and stepped into the darkness. Standing inside for a few moments, he couldn't help but notice things were very different. His heart wasn't pounding and his breathing was calm. Maybe he was just getting used to it.

He opened the door carefully into the corridor and the familiar light bolted into the cupboard, illuminating the rubbish stored inside.

He saw carpeted floor, modern coats and bags, polystyrene ceiling tiles. And Mrs Jameson standing staring at him with a stern look on her face.

"Why are you in there?" she snapped angrily.

Eddie glanced about him, knowing that his attempt to reach Charlotte had failed. His shoulders slumped and he hung his head, trying to hide behind his hair.

"Dunno," he mumbled. "Just wanted a look, I suppose."

"This is so disappointing, Eddie," she said, sighing. "And after you did so well this morning. You know you are not supposed to go snooping in cupboards. You had better come with me."

The boys (and one girl) playing football outside wondered where Eddie had got to, when he failed to turn up for the lunchtime game. He had to eat his packed lunch in Mr Evans' office, under the solemn watch of the headteacher who had spoken to him about "responsibilities", "health and safety" and "following the rules of the school".

Eddie knew what disappointment was. He was even a bit sad he had let his teacher down after his triumph in the classroom. He was also sad he had not been able to reach Charlotte and that the magic of the door seemed to have gone.

CHAPTER 15

Despite his telling off for going into the cupboard, Eddie was beginning to enjoy school more and more. Over the next couple of weeks he became firm friends with Alfie and Ethan and he started to try harder in class. He wasn't so bothered about writing but he knew he was good at maths, and was even starting to make an effort to make his work neat and presentable. Mrs Jameson seemed pleased with him and he had to admit that this had started to feel good.

Eddie's mother noticed the change in him and was getting a bit more enthusiastic about school herself, dropping him off on time in the morning and collecting him as close to 3.15pm as she possibly could, bearing in mind she always drove up and down waiting for someone to exit one of the parking spaces close by so that she didn't have to walk far.

She had also got herself a job, working in the Tesco Express serving customers and even managing to turn up on time every morning. Her cheerful face and friendly smile proved popular with the locals and the manager of the shop was very pleased with his new worker.

"Things are looking up for us, Eddie," she said one morning, as he stood with his school bag by the front door waiting for her to finish putting jam on his sandwich.

"Yes mum," he answered, with a slight grin. He tucked the plastic bag with his outdoor trainers into his bag – there was no way he was going to miss playing lunchtime football now.

He loved the friendly arguments and the excitement of scoring goals. He even tolerated allowing a girl to play on his side. Alfie and Ethan didn't seem to mind, in fact they got on quite well with some of the girls in the class.

Eddie was now feeling different about his life. He was still hooked on his computer sessions in the evenings, but he had noticed that other things were interesting too. Football at break time. Harry Potter books. Feeling quite proud of himself after solving some difficult maths problems.

There was one dark cloud on his horizon, though. Charlotte and what had happened to her after their attempt to come back into the 21st Century. Eddie was still concerned and worried.

His attempt to go back and see her had ended up with him spending a lunchtime in Mr Evans' office and he really didn't want to chance that again. Each time he passed the door, he brushed his hand against the sandtimer and was forced to admit the magical electricity was no longer there.

He started to accept that he would never see her again and that the whole thing had just been a weird day dream. Maybe it was time to forget Charlotte and that sadder, more lonely time in his life.

Then one afternoon, two weeks after he had last seen Charlotte, Alfie's mum, Mrs Hall, approached Eddie's mother on the playground, as the children were being dismissed by their teacher. Eddie watched warily as Mrs Hall walked up to them, weaving through the crowd of parents, pupils, bags and toddlers all milling around in the busy confusion.

"Hello," said Mrs Hall, as Alfie stood grinning behind them.

"Yes?" answered Eddie's mother abruptly, spinning around to face her and bracing herself for any complaint about her son.

Mrs Hall smiled warmly and placed a hand behind her on Alfie's shoulder, pulling him next to her.

"Alfie here and Eddie seem to have struck up a friendship in the past couple of weeks," she continued, looking fondly down at her son who was nodding encouragingly at his friend.

"And?" said Eddie's mother, glaring at her son, expecting to hear that he had done something wrong.

"Well, we were wondering if he would like to come round tomorrow for tea. Would that be OK? I can pick them up and you can collect him at, say, 6pm?"

Eddie's mum's mouth dropped open in surprise and she quickly shut it again, a little embarrassed that she had answered so rudely. She produced her brightest smile and nodded energetically, hoping to make the other woman forget the way she had replied.

"Ooh, that would be fantastic, wouldn't it, Eddie? Thank you so much. I am sure he would love to come, wouldn't you?" His mother looked down encouragingly at him as Eddie nodded. The two boys grinned at each other and the mothers made quick arrangements about addresses and times. Eddie felt on top of the world.

The next day it came as a surprise when, as he brushed past the cupboard to get to his bag, Eddie felt the familiar electric static that had first made him think about touching the handle. He almost jumped back in shock and the other boys, who were also getting their outdoor trainers, laughed.

"Woah," laughed Ethan. "That was some static. I almost heard it crackle!"

"Yes," answered Eddie. "It sometimes does that when mum has washed my jumper in a different washing soap."

He looked down and knew he was lying. He had heard his mum talk about static in the washing and was now using it as an excuse to avoid having to explain to the others what had happened. He was convinced they wouldn't believe him.

Also, the idea of chancing another trip into that other world was a little scary as he wasn't even sure if Charlotte was real. The memories were now hazy and dim and he struggled to remember what she even looked like. It made him feel a little sick and odd. And he didn't want to end up in more trouble at school like the last time he had attempted to go back to her world.

But, despite everything he told himself, the magnetic pull of the silver handle continued to reach out to him each time he passed it. Even though Eddie tried to deny it, the pull was getting stronger and stronger each time. And the distant and faded memory of Charlotte's shocked face when she stepped out to face the angry voice of her teacher still haunted him.

CHAPTER 16

The day of the visit to Alfie's house arrived dull and damp. It was now early October and the clouds hung low in the sky and the air had a nip of cold. However, Eddie felt warm with anticipation. All day at school, he felt a tinge of excitement, and a few nerves, at the thought of visiting Alfie's house after school.

At his previous school, the other children had avoided him, wary of his sullen glances and the way he could get angry very quickly. When Eddie got angry, you didn't want to get in his way. So they made sure they stayed out of it. It was so much more fun to be in the centre of things and have other children to play with and talk to, admitted Eddie.

The minutes ticked by slowly and Eddie struggled to concentrate on his lessons but finally it was 3.15pm and the children spilled out on to the playground like a river bursting from a dam. Mrs Hall was standing, chatting to some other parents, and her face lit up into a smile when she saw the two boys standing next to eachother, bags hooked over their shoulders.

"Come on, you two," she laughed. "Let's go!"

Alfie lived just around the corner from the school. The two boys trailed after Alfie's mum, whacking eachother playfully with their bags and kicking up little stones on the way. They trotted down the main road and then turned into a cul-de-sac opposite the Rose and Crown pub. Small, modern terraced houses circled the road. Alfie's was the second on the right and they piled in, dumping their bags on the carpet and heading straight into the kitchen for a drink.

Through the window, Eddie could see a small garden. Several footballs lay scattered about as if abandoned mid-match, and a black and white goalpost held pride of place.

"So," said Mrs Hall, as she moved their drinking glasses from the table into the dishwasher. "What are you two going to do now?"

"Well, what about a quick game on the computer?" said Alfie, turning to Eddie, his eyebrows raised in a question mark.

"Yeah, great," said Eddie, thinking that an afternoon playing computer games sounded like fun.

Mrs Hall frowned a little and leant back against the kitchen surface.

"Only half an hour then," she said firmly.

Eddie looked at her, confused. What did she mean "only half an hour"? He spent hours each evening playing games and no one ever commented or tried to stop him. He looked sideways at Alfie, who was still munching on a biscuit, looking completely unconcerned.

"OK mum, half an hour," he answered, getting up from his stool and shaking the crumbs on to the floor.

"And sweep those up before you go!"

Eddie's eyes widened in surprise as his friend went to a long cupboard in the corner of the kitchen and fetched a dustpan and brush and started sweeping up the crumbs carefully, before putting them in the bin. Eddie never helped his mum, but here was Alfie doing it without a single moan. It made him think a little. Mrs Hall picked up a cloth and wiped the table, before waving the two boys off with a flick of her hand and a friendly smile.

"Go on, you two! Have fun!"

The rest of the afternoon was spent playing on Alfie's computer then scampering around the garden practising tackles and goal shoots. Eddie loved every minute, despite being only allowed on the computer for half an hour. The two boys were exhausted when Mrs Hall called them in for their tea.

Later, full of chicken, chips and carrots, followed by a dough-nut, the boys sat on Alfie's bed looking through a book on "Football Greats". As they thumbed through the pages, Eddie thought about Charlotte and how different her world was to his. He wondered if he could tell his friend, if he would understand.

"Have you ever wondered if it was possible to travel back in time?" Eddie asked, as Alfie looked at a page on "The ten best footballers of all time". Alfie briefly glanced up at his friend.

"Not really,' he mumbled. "Would be fun though. A bit like Dr Who."

"What would you say if I told you I know someone who has," continued Eddie, carefully.

"Has what?"

"Travelled back in time."

Alfie leaned back on the wall, pushing a cushion behind him.

"I would say they were a complete weirdo," he replied, firmly.

So Eddie abandoned any thoughts of telling Alfie what had happened. Is that what he was, then? A weirdo? Even if he was, at this moment he was quite a happy one.

CHAPTER 17

It was the first lesson of the next day. English. Two days had now passed since the static had flashed so dramatically towards Eddie, startling Ethan.

Mrs Jameson introduced the lesson's task, saying she was really excited to tell them they were going to enter a competition that had been set up by the museum in the nearby large town, Fordingham. The museum was encouraging children to think about how people lived in the past and write an autobiographical account of a child from a different age. The entries had to focus on life from Anglo Saxon times to the Second World War.

"Does anyone know what 'autobiographical' means?" asked the teacher, scanning the classroom.

As usual, Sarah Norman knew exactly what it meant.

"It's when you write something about your own life," she answered confidently.

"Exactly," said Mrs Jameson. "So your task is to write something about the past from the *point of view* of a child in that time. Imagine you are that child and you are writing about your daily life at home or at school. It needs to be about five hundred words long and full of powerful sentences and accurate historical information. What do you think you will need to do before you start?"

The children had lots of suggestions: research on the computer, research in books, reading stories from that time, looking at paintings and so on.

Mrs Jameson brought the class together after their enthusias-tic conversation about how to find out information about his-tory and the way that people lived in years gone by.

"So, do you want to know what the top prize is?" she asked the class. They all roared: "Yes!"

"Well, first prize is…" she looked carefully at the information leaflet she held in her hand. "Your story will be printed onto a poster and displayed in the Fordingham Town Museum as part of its 'Young Lives in the Past' exhibition. And you will win £100!"

The children were excited, unable to believe that any of them could possibly see their writing in print, viewed by the dozens of adults and children who visited the museum each day.

Eddie's mind was in a whirl. He knew, for once, that his writ-ing would be more accurate and real than anybody else's could possibly be. Excited, he knew that he stood a good chance of winning – if only he was able to put down his ideas on paper. He suddenly wished he had paid more attention in English lessons.

Maybe Charlotte would help him; she seemed pretty clever and was probably brilliant at writing and stuff like that. The thought of winning a whole £100 filled him with enthusiasm. He started to think what he could do with all that money. There was a new football game that had just come out: FIFA 2018. It looked like fun.

He decided he would try to travel back to see Charlotte now that the magic seemed to have returned. He would also be able to find out what had happened to her and hopefully stop her anxious face from haunting his thoughts. He would finally find out if it had all been real or just his imagination playing tricks on him. And there was no time like the present, before his fears and doubts got the better of him.

Eddie thought about how he could get into the cupboard without anyone finding out. Going in at breaktimes would be difficult, as the teachers were keeping an eye on him now. It would also be difficult to chance it when his friends were around. He certainly didn't want them to know about his scheme, as they would then think he was odd. He didn't want to go back to those days.

As the clock ticked steadily through the English lesson, the children worked hard at their research notes, looking up on the computers how children used to live in Tudor and Victorian times. Some investigated the difficult days of the Second World War and others wondered what it might have been like to have been an Anglo Saxon child, scared of the Viking invaders.

Eddie got up and asked Mrs Jameson if he could change his reading book. The children were allowed to go to the library to change books when they had finished them. She was busily helping a pupil to search for "children in Anglo Saxon times" and glanced briefly at Eddie before saying: "OK then, but be quick".

He walked quietly out of the classroom and into the corridor. He should have carried on to the library, but instead he brushed his hand against the little brown door. Looking down at the handle, he saw the grains of sand had seeped further into the bottom half of the hourglass. Eddie knew this time that it was not his imagination and that the sand had really moved. He struggled to grasp what it could mean, but he had to move quickly as the familiar electricity crackled against his hand. With a furtive glance around him, he grabbled the handle, shot inside and shut the door behind him.

When Eddie opened it again, he noticed a strange, pale light echoing across the now-familiar tiled corridor. Instead of children's voices shrieking outside, he could hear the steady rhythm of young voices repeating lines in the classroom ahead of him. He had done it. He was back.

He crossed the corridor and stood on his tiptoes to look into the classroom. A stern-looking woman was standing at the front with a long, dark brown dress and her hair tightly pulled up into a bun on the back of her head. She had small half-moon glasses balanced on the end of her nose and she was tapping at the board with her stick as she chanted.

"Incline thine ear unto wisdom, and apply thine heart to understanding," said the teacher, flicking her stick against each word as she said it.

The children sat and scraped loudly at small boards they held in their hands. The squeaking of the pencils, which made strange marks on the boards, made Eddie hold his hands to his ears. It was horrible.

He then glanced around at the children, who all looked frozen and who gazed longingly at a stove in the corner of the room, which appeared to give out a little heat.

When Eddie looked through the high windows into the playground beyond, he could see the treetops were covered in white. It had obviously been snowing. So it was now deep winter in this school, although in Eddie's time it was only the beginning of October. And it was clearly very, very cold. Some of the children were blowing on their fingers to keep them warm enough for writing. Eddie felt nothing, not cold or warm. Clearly the temperature did not affect him at all.

"And you, Jeremy Blacksmith, what have you got to say for yourself now?" said the teacher, turning to face one of the corners of the room.

Eddie had to stand high on his toes to peer around the edge to his left and spot, standing on a small stool, a boy with a strange hat on his head. It was like an elf's hat, except much longer and pointier, and it had a big D written on it. The boy looked very miserable and had snot dribbling down from his nose. His clothes looked tatty and had lots of patches where someone had tried to sew holes together.

"Do you think you can continue your Bible verse without making such a terrible mess of your letters? Do you think you can find it within yourself to do the task in hand adequately?" demanded the stern lady.

The little boy snivelled and shivered as he was at the opposite end of the room to the stove. He nodded quietly and wiped his nose on his sleeve, where it left a silver trail.

"Well, return to your seat then and let this be a lesson to you," said the teacher.

The little boy climbed sadly down from the stool and staggered back to his seat, his small legs unstable from the effort of standing for so long on the stool and holding his head up to prevent the hat from toppling off. In a strange way, Eddie was suddenly reminded of Ethan and his cheerful admission that he had dyslexia and Mrs Jameson's careful supervision of him and his work in class.

Eddie was shocked. He felt outraged that this little boy should be treated like this. They had been taught about rights, human rights, at school, but then he had a sneaking suspicion that maybe they hadn't existed in Victorian times.

He reminded himself that he had an important job to do and scanned around the class to see where Charlotte was and work out how he could attract her attention without her getting into trouble.

The girls all sat on one side, the boys on the other. That made it easier to search all the pinched, cold, unhappy faces in front of him.

He looked each line up and down several times, taking in the thin lips, patched-up clothes and sad faces.

But Charlotte was not there.

CHAPTER 18

E ddie looked and looked again. No matter how many times he stared at the young faces in front of him, he still couldn't see her. Where on earth was she?

He looked down at his fingers, thinking it was just over two weeks since he had been through the cupboard. Last time, he had gone back the next day and Charlotte had told him that a week had passed in her time. So if he had now returned more than two weeks later, that would mean... Eddie was quick at maths and did the calculation rapidly in his head. He knew, obviously, that there were seven days in a week. That would mean, he concentrated hard, that around sixteen weeks had passed since he last saw Charlotte, towards the end of September. How may weeks in a month? Yes, around four. So that would mean around four months. October, November, December, January. It must be around the middle of January. That would explain why there was snow outside. It was in the middle of winter for Charlotte.

But she wasn't here, at school. So there was only one solution. He had to find her. He needed her to help him write his competition entry. But he had no idea where to start.

Slumping down onto the tiled floor, Eddie went back through their conversations. He tried to find any clue, any hint as to where she could be. Her face swam in front of him, with her pale skin and dark eyes. Her hair tied back with that white ribbon and her white apron-like dress over her dark clothing.

He then remembered her gentle, painful cough. If she had been coughing like that in September, when it was warmer, maybe she had got worse as the weather had become colder.

He stood up and looked at the children sitting in the classroom, still scraping away with their scratchy pencils on those strange boards.

They were dressed in more layers of clothing than they had been before and several were still rubbing hands together to warm them up. It was clearly freezing cold in there. He had a sudden, horrible thought. Perhaps Charlotte had died? He suspected they didn't have great doctors in Victorian times.

Obviously, thought Eddie, he couldn't ask any of her friends, as none of them had been able to see him. In fact it seemed as if Charlotte was the only one who was aware of him being there. It was hopeless.

He slipped back down on to the floor again, thinking he might as well give up and go back into the cupboard and return to the busy, bustling school he had just left and write his museum entry all on his own. Eddie could see the £100 disappearing before his eyes.

Suddenly, he looked up and gave a little grin. He remembered. She had said something about her parents being bakers. He was sure of it. Bakers made bread, he knew that. And so they must have some sort of shop and to have a shop, it must be somewhere near the centre of the village.

He would just have to go and find it. He was not going to give up. He was going to find her.

Eddie stood up and walked to the end of the corridor, where the door led to the outside area. He pushed the door open, still wondering how he could touch and move things in a world where he didn't really seem to exist. Outside, everything was covered by a white dusting of snow. He was prepared to be frozen as he was only wearing his school uniform and had no coat with him. However, once outside, the temperature was the same. Not hot, not cold.

He looked around himself to try and judge where he should

go. The houses that surrounded St Paul's in his own time were now replaced by trees and bushes. This little village was a small town in his own time.

He could see the railings at the front of the school playground and thought about how they had been replaced in modern times by a high metal fence, which had a security-locked door leading out onto the busy main road.

Here, there was just a low brick wall with iron railings above and a small wooden gate. The road appeared to be empty of any cars or traffic. Cars? He reminded himself that things were very different in this world. Maybe they had horses and carts? Charlotte had said her dad had heard of a new invention that used motors to power carts, but had never seen one herself, clearly. Cars were obviously not a common sight in 1898. In fact, he thought, now that it was January, it must actually be 1899.

Eddie walked over to the gate and peered up and down the street. It was paved, but covered in dirty muck. The snow had been mashed up into the mud and it looked like a brown mess. There were buildings, and some of them he even recognised.

He saw in the distance the swinging pub sign for the Rose and Crown. Another building, which was now the Tesco Express, had "Village Stores" written in white lettering above the door. Gaps between these buildings had since been filled in with new, modern houses and it was difficult to connect what he saw now with his life in the 21st Century.

There were one or two people going in and out of the store and others hurrying down the side of the road, the women lifting their long skirts to avoid getting covered in mud.

As he was staring about, trying to get his bearings, he heard a rumble and a loud clatter. Around the corner appeared a horse, pulling a cart behind it, with a man holding the reins and a long whip. The cart trotted down the street and clattered noisily past Eddie, making him jump backwards. It disappeared into the distance, throwing up clods of mud behind it.

Eddie opened the gate and stepped out into the street. As he walked along he stared about in amazement. This world was similar, but so different.   A woman walked past him, stepping unconsciously aside to avoid bumping into him as if guided by a mysterious force. She had a hat on which was tied under her chin and shaded her face as it had a sort of rim, which stuck right out. A man, dressed in a thick jacket and cap, crossed over to the other side of the road, his feet covered in mud by the time he reached the other side. He hardly seemed to notice.

And then he saw it. Down the road, opposite The Rose and Crown pub, there was a small, shabby-looking building set back slightly from the street.

It had a sign which said "Simmonds Bakery" on the front in peeling letters.

He had found it. That must be Charlotte's home.

CHAPTER 19

As he walked along the street towards the bakery, the odd horse and cart rumbling past, Eddie understood that the cold couldn't touch him. It was as if he was a ghost drifting through this strange landscape. It sent a shudder through him, reminding him how he had thought he might have been a ghost when he first met Charlotte.

He now knew he wasn't, but he couldn't work out exactly what he was in this strange world. He had to put that out of his mind and concentrate on finding out where Charlotte was. He decided that if he couldn't find her, he would close the door on this adventure and not return. He just wouldn't make much effort with the competition, as he knew writing wasn't his strong point. Eddie thought sadly about what £100 would look like in his hands.

The bakery was now in front of him and he paused, looking up at the building. He glanced up and down the street and over to the other side of the road towards the pub.

Looking back to Simmonds Bakery, he realised that this building no longer existed in his own time. It was now the street that led to Alfie's house, which he had visited the day before. He briefly wondered when, and why, the building had been pulled down. He remembered how he and Alfie had swung their bags at each other, laughing and happy, as they walked like phantoms of the future, through the space now filled by the building standing solidly in front of him.

He pushed the door open and went inside. A woman turned around sharply and looked straight at him and he froze. However, she was not looking at him, but at the open door. She shuffled over, her long skirt sweeping the floor, and he quickly stood to one side.

"Oh, this cold," she muttered. "Why on earth does the door open on its own like this? We must keep the cold out."

Eddie glanced around, but there was no one else in the shop. She must have been talking to herself. She shut the door with a little annoyed mutter and went back to the wooden counter where she had been standing.

Loaves of bread were piled on shelves behind, and she had a book open on the counter, an ink pen lying next to it. She picked up the pen and carried on making little notes in the book.

The shop had two windows looking out on to the street, and a wooden floor. Flour dusted the counter and the woman's hands were coated in a layer of white. On one side there was a big oven with a heavy metal door. Eddie could see it must be warm in the shop because the woman was not wearing the heavy clothes he had seen on people outside. There were no lights in the shop and the air was dull and musty. She had no idea he was standing in front of her.

Behind the counter was a door and Eddie wondered if that might lead him to Charlotte. Maybe the family lived behind the shop and she was in there somewhere. He couldn't imagine she would be off school for no reason as she had told him how much she liked to learn.

He walked around the counter, knowing he had to open the door and that the woman would wonder, again, what was going on. But he had no choice. He had come this far, it would be stupid not to finish what he had started.

"Hmmn," muttered the woman, her pen scribbling away in the book. "Mrs Dawson brought in two loaves for baking this morning and has not paid yet. I must get Jack to ask her for the money."

Eddie couldn't understand what she was talking about.

Surely she would bake the bread rather than other people bring their loaves to her for baking. He would have to ask Charlotte.

As she was busily writing, Eddie grabbed his chance, and reached for the handle. Quickly he opened the door and scurried into the dark hallway behind it.

The woman looked up, startled, and glanced around the shop. As he stood in the darkness, he saw her silhouette in the doorway, peering from the shop into the hallway in confusion.

"Charlotte, my love," she called. "Is that you? Do you need something?'

A feeble voice drifted through the building from upstairs.

"No mother, thank you."

"Well, tell me if you feel any worse," she answered. "How strange," she added, shutting the door with her foot.

So she was here, thought Eddie. He then heard a terrible, rasping cough coming from above. Charlotte was here, Eddie thought, but she clearly wasn't very well.

He walked quickly ahead into the gloom.

CHAPTER 20

The hallway was dark and had brown wallpaper, which was peeling off in places. In the dim light, Eddie could make out some stairs, which went off from the right-hand side. He moved forward and crept up them, not knowing where he was going or what he might find.

Once he reached the top, he could see a small landing with three dark brown doors, which were all firmly shut. He stopped and listened. A dry, rasping cough came from behind the door on his left, so he moved towards it and put his ear against the wood. The cough came again, this time quieter. The sound was definitely coming from inside. He opened the door, which creaked slightly as light seeped into the hallway.

And there, lying on the bed, was Charlotte.

Her eyes were shut and she was holding a handkerchief in her hand, which lay on the bedcovers. Her dark hair was fanned out over the thin pillow and her skin was white and covered with a film of sweat.

A glass of water was on a small wooden table next to her bed and the curtains were tightly shut against the light, but they were worn and thin and some of the day managed to steal into the dark room. There was a wooden chest in one corner and a table and chair along another wall. A small fire burned in the fireplace, fighting against the cold air outside.

As she coughed again, holding her hand to her chest in pain, her eyes flew open and she saw him standing by the door.

He could see the shock on her face change into a small smile which spread across her mouth, but which clearly took a lot of effort.

"Ah, you have come," she said in a whisper. "I hoped you would. It has been a long time since you were here last."

It was as if she had known he would return and was expecting him.

"Well, you weren't at school," said Eddie, hardly knowing what to say to her.

"No, I'm not at school," she managed a sad, quiet chuckle.

He shut the door carefully, so that the woman downstairs, whom he presumed was Charlotte's mother, wouldn't hear her daughter talking to a nobody. He then went over to the girl and stood awkwardly.

"It isn't appropriate," she said, "for a boy to enter a girl's room like this. But I don't suppose anyone will ever know." She patted her hand lightly on the bed. "Sit down here."

Eddie, who didn't like taking orders from anyone, sat down gingerly on the thin, worn bedcovers and cleared his throat.

"What is wrong with you?"

"I have asthma," she said simply. "And it has worsened into a chest complaint, as you can see. I have never had anything as bad as this before."

"Have the doctors been to see you?" asked Eddie, all thoughts of her helping with the museum competition having disappeared at the sight of her lying there so unwell.

"Ha!" she scoffed. "My parents hardly have money for doctors. But one did come, and said I needed to rest. I have been doing a lot of that but it is getting no better."

She was suddenly caught up in a coughing fit that shook her whole thin, weak body. Eddie was shocked and picked up the glass and awkwardly held it out to her, having no idea what to do or how to help. Gradually she managed to stop coughing and lay silent, exhausted.

"They just said to rest? What about medicine? Surely there's something you could take?" Eddie had no idea what, as he had never had any serious illnesses himself.

"Well, they have tried tobacco," said Charlotte, her eyes still shut from the effort of coughing.

"Tobacco? What do you mean?"

"Smoking tobacco is supposed to help, but it doesn't. It just makes me cough even more. It is horrible."

Eddie gasped in horror. He put the glass down and leaned over to look at her face.

"Cigarettes?" he exclaimed. "But they kill you. They give you lung cancer. Everyone knows that. My mum used to smoke but gave up after seeing a programme on what people's lungs look like when they have smoked for a few years."

"A programme? What's that? Is it something on your magic box?"

"On the TV... oh never mind. Just don't. Don't ever smoke tobacco again, I am sure it would make your asthma much worse, not better."

"Well, there is not much else they can do. My parents fear it is bad air, but they have no money to take me anywhere else." She shut her eyes again and breathed out carefully.

A small tear trickled from her eye and dripped down her cheek on to the stained pillow.

"I fear my days are numbered. There was so much I wanted to do. And I am worried about my poor parents, who have already lost two children..." She didn't need to say the rest.

Eddie gulped and desperately tried to not show her that he was nearly crying himself. He felt so powerless. This was far worse than a normal cold, even he could see that.

"So, tell me, how is it in your time? Make me forget how bad I feel," she said.

"Well, there are more cars and houses, that's for certain," answered Eddie, trying to lighten the mood a little. "Did you get punished that last time I saw you, when they caught you coming out of the cupboard?"

"Oh yes. Six strikes, on the hand," she said, not even seeming to realise how awful Eddie would find that idea. "But I suppose I deserved it for being disobedient."

Eddie thought about what he could tell her. He remembered their discussion about cars and she listened quietly, breathing heavily, as he described modern-day cars with their top speeds of more than 100mph.

He talked about being able to travel from one end of the country to the other in a matter of hours, and how mini-computers could even direct you to stop you taking a wrong turn.

Finally, his lively explanations trailing out, he thought back to the little boy, Jeremy Blacksmith, who had been standing so forlornly in the classroom. He pictured the hat on his head with the large D written on it.

"Can I ask you something?" he whispered. Charlotte nodded.

"Why was a boy in your class wearing a big hat with a D on it? What does it mean?"

The girl opened her eyes a little and drew breath.

"It means 'dunce'," she breathed, so quietly he could hardly hear her. "It means he is being punished for being stupid."

Ethan's bright face with its friendly grin and freckles swam in front of Eddie's eyes. There was no way anyone would ever call him stupid, that was certain. Poor Jeremy Blacksmith, thought Eddie.

Charlotte shut her eyes and swallowed painfully. As Eddie watched her, he realised that he actually cared about what happened to her and wished there was something he could do.

Charlotte's breathing became quieter and Eddie knew she was asleep. He sat staring at his friend, who was fading away in front of him.

She had been so full of life and so desperate to learn and do things, he could not believe it had come to this. He was angry with the useless doctors who suggested ridiculous treatments like smoking cigarettes and her stupid parents who didn't see that they needed to do more for their daughter.

He felt himself becoming angry, angrier than he had ever been before. But instead of using his "strategies", he allowed the anger to spread through his body as he watched her short, pained breathing.

Eddie let himself be angry as he sensed it was all right to feel like this, for once. It made him feel more powerful and made him understand that he could, and should, do something. There was only one person who could help her and that was Eddie. This was his moment to think, to plan and to act. He got up and looked one last time at her sleeping face.

"I am going home," he said. "To my magic box to find a cure for you, Charlotte. And I will be back with it. And you are going to get better. Just hold on a few more days and I will show you."

And with those words, he stood up, went to the door and left.

CHAPTER 21

Mrs Jameson was taking the register when she remembered that the children had to change for PE. They all rushed outside to get their PE bags and quickly change into shorts and T shirts.

Eddie couldn't get the picture of Charlotte lying, desperately ill on her bed, out of his mind. Sadness seemed to colour everything and the other boys' laughter grated on him. They just thought he was being miserable and moody again, but there was no way he could even begin to tell them what had happened.

"Ethan," said Mrs Jameson. "Don't forget your inhaler when you go out."

"I won't," said Ethan happily, going to his teacher's desk and getting his blue, plastic inhaler from a box.

Eddie watched him closely, thinking about how lucky he was to have an inhaler, which meant he could join in with sports without much of a worry.

He thought how great it would be if Charlotte could somehow get an inhaler like that one. Maybe he could steal it? The thought churned around in his head through the games lesson as the children learned throwing and catching skills on the playground under the careful direction of their teacher.

As the balls whizzed around him, Eddie struggled to stay focused and often missed easy catches, much to the annoyance of his team.

The lesson finished and the children, red-faced, exhausted

and happy, trundled back into the classroom to get changed. Ethan went and put his inhaler back in the box and Eddie kept a close eye on Mrs Jameson as she put it back in her cupboard. He had never seen Ethan actually use the inhaler and thought to himself, it must still be quite full. That would be good for Charlotte.

When school was finished, prayers said and bags collected, the children got ready to go outside with Mrs Jameson to meet their parents.

Everyone was shoving to get outside first, with their teacher leading the way. Jostling and pushing eachother playfully, the class made it out onto the playground where the parents were chatting and waiting expectantly. Eddie looked around quickly and saw, as was still sometimes the case, his mother had not yet arrived.

"Mrs Jameson," he asked. The teacher absent-mindedly looked down at him as a parent stood waiting to speak to her about something.

"Er, yes, quickly Eddie – what is it?"

"I have left my book in the classroom. Can I just run back and get it?"

"OK, but be quick as you're not supposed to be in the classroom on your own." And then she turned to the waiting parent to see what they wanted to say.

Eddie dashed back through the door, down the corridor and into the classroom. Peering out of the windows into the corridor, he checked no one was watching, and pulled open the cupboard door. If anyone caught him now, he would be in for it.

His hands shaking, he grabbed the box and fumbled the clasps open. He grasped the inhaler and stuffed it into his bag. He shut the box and put it back before shutting the cupboard and running back out of the classroom.

"Did you find it?" asked Mrs Jameson.

"Find what?" said Eddie, looking around for his mother.

"Your book!"

"Oh, yeah. I did thanks. Here's my mum now!" And she appeared at just the right time, for once, to rescue Eddie from any more awkward questions. He picked up his bag, which held the stolen inhaler, and happily jogged to his mother.

"Hey babes," she said, ruffling his hair. "Fancy a pizza? I've just been paid!"

And so the two of them left as Mrs Jameson went back into her classroom.

When she entered, she noticed the cupboard door was slightly ajar, so went over to check it. She opened it and quickly looked inside. The medication box had been placed on the third shelf, not the second one where she always put it. And one of the clasps was undone. She pulled off the lid and checked inside. A frown froze on her face. The inhaler was gone.

CHAPTER 22

The computer whirred quickly into life as Eddie sat in his darkening room, having sat through a meal at Pizza Hut, pretending to enjoy it, but really wanting to get home and start finding out how he could help Charlotte.

He could almost feel the inhaler burning a hole in his bag. Eddie knew he had stolen it and he would be in big trouble if anyone found out, but he persuaded himself that he had done something very wrong to actually do something that was very good.

He would have to somehow get back to Charlotte before anyone discovered the inhaler and found out that he was a thief. His future at the school would be destroyed if his teachers, and classmates, knew what he had done, and somehow he didn't want that to happen. Never before had he cared about school, but he was beginning to really like Alfie, Ethan and the lunchtime football games. Even Mrs Jameson wasn't too bad, and writing was beginning to become a little easier for him.

He took the inhaler out of his bag and studied it. The small machine was blue, with a sort of round cartridge pushed up inside it. When he had seen children using it, they had held it in their mouths, pressed the bottom and sort of breathed in. He was pretty sure he would be able to show Charlotte how to do that. He had a sudden panic that maybe he wouldn't be able to take things across into her time, but comforted himself with the thought that he managed to carry his shoes and clothes with him, so perhaps the inhaler wouldn't be any different. It was only taking things back from Charlotte's time to his that seemed to be impossible.

The internet fired up as his fingers flew across the keyboard. If there was one thing Eddie could do, that was type quickly. He had certainly had a lot of practice.

The light outside was fading and the bright screen filled up the room with a comforting glow as Eddie asked Google for how many pushes on the inhaler Charlotte needed to take to make herself better.

For an acute asthma attack. Give your child one puff from the inhaler. Wait 15–30 seconds, then give another one. You can give them a maximum of 10 puffs, waiting 15–30 seconds between puffs.

So, she needed about ten puffs, he thought. But would that make her better? She certainly seemed a lot sicker than the children he had seen puffing on their inhalers at his old school. What was it she was suffering from? Her white face lying back on the thin, poor pillow came back to him. What was it she had said? Eddie racked his brains. The words swam around and he tried to catch them, to remember them. It was very important that he remembered exactly what she said.

"A chest something," he muttered, trying to grasp that final word to complete the puzzle. "A chest... COMPLAINT! That was it!"

He quickly typed it into Google, suspicious that it was not an illness he had heard described before. As he typed in the words "What is a chest..." Google helpfully came up with the suggestion "What is a chest infection?" Eddie knew he had heard of that and clicked on an NHS page, which gave advice.

The next hour passed quickly as Eddie read through the internet suggestions on chest infections in asthmatic people and the symptoms he had seen Charlotte suffering – the temperature, the terrible coughing, her obvious pain and how weak she was. And he looked carefully at the modern, life-saving treatment that was used to help people.

Antibiotics. That was what doctors gave to people with really bad chest infections. Why hadn't she been given them, he wondered? She had said her family wasn't rich, but antibiotics didn't seem expensive. Maybe they didn't have antibiotics in Victorian times.

Another tapping search showed him that antibiotics hadn't been discovered until...1928 by a man called Alexander Fleming. That was thirty years after he had found himself visiting Charlotte.

She didn't stand a chance, he thought sadly, living in a time that thought cigarettes were a cure for a serious chest illness. He had seen how sick she was and how she believed she did not have long to live and he carefully and deviously designed a plan, which would take a lot of daring, and luck, if it was to succeed.

Because now this really was a matter of life or death.

CHAPTER 23

Eddie rummaged around under his bed and found, covered in dust and bits of food, which had been kicked underneath, his old hot water bottle. Their previous house had been cold and damp and the hot water bottle had been a way of warming up cold sheets on a freezing night.

He grabbed the rubbery bottle and slipped silently downstairs, glancing at his mum through the sitting room door. She was happily watching a comedy programme, chuckling to herself over some joke and tapping on the rim of her wine glass.

Tiptoeing past, he went into the kitchen, boiled a kettle and filled the bottle up with steaming water before creeping back up to his room. He put on his dressing gown, and crawled into bed, clasping the wobbling bottle tight and pulling the duvet right up around himself.

The heat was almost unbearable and soon Eddie was sweating uncontrollably, with droplets forming nicely on his forehead. He practised a few little, hoarse coughs until he felt he could carry it off perfectly. The scene was set and it was time to pull off the performance of his life.

"MUM!" he yelled as loudly as he could, hoping the TV wouldn't drown out his calls.

"Yes, babes," came the voice from the bottom of the hallway. "What do you want?"

"Come up here. I don't feel well," answered Eddie, trying to sound feeble, but also needing her to hear him clearly.

Footsteps plodded up the stairs and his mother's face appeared at the door of the bedroom, with a broad smile, which soon turned to concern when she saw her son's flushed face and heard his dry, painful cough.

"Goodness me, what on earth is wrong with you?" she said, running over to him and peering closely at his red, sweating face. She placed her hand on his forehead and jumped back.

"You are burning up! When did this start? You were fine when we were having a pizza."

Eddie coughed a little more, holding his hand to his chest as Charlotte had done. He tried to look as ill as he could, turning his head painfully to look at his mother.

"I have felt a bit ill for a few days, but didn't want to say anything," he muttered, adding another little cough for effect. "But now I feel terrible. My chest is so painful it hurts to breathe. I feel like I am dying or something."

Eddie was anxiously trying to remember all the symptoms he had seen Charlotte suffering. He hoped he hadn't overdone it.

"Well, I am sure you will survive," said his mum, with a little grin. "Nobody dies from a little cough and temperature. I will take you to the doctor first thing tomorrow and get some medicine. I'll get you some water and pain-killers and hopefully you will have a good night's sleep."

As the sun finally set, Eddie settled back into his bed, the hot water bottle now cooling and his body temperature returning to normal.

He knew he would have to be up early tomorrow to make sure he put the next part of his plan into action. One day in modern times was a week in Charlotte's time, so he desperately hoped that, if he acted as quickly as he could, he wouldn't be too late to save her.

CHAPTER 24

The sunlight crept silently through the curtains and threw its sharp lines across Eddie's face. Everything was still and silent as he woke slowly up, remembering that it was crucial that he acted the moment he awoke.

The small alarm clock showed it was still very early, around 6.30am. The day was just beginning for him, but Charlotte could be taking her last breaths in her time, so distant and so far from his own reality.

Yawning quietly, Eddie stumbled out of his bed and retrieved the hot water bottle from the bottom of his bed, where it had got wrapped up in the ends of his duvet.

The corridor outside was silent and his mother's door was firmly shut. She usually slept quite late as her shift at Tesco's didn't start until after the beginning of school. It was usually about 7.45am before she finally dragged herself out of bed and stirred into action.

Eddie went downstairs to repeat the previous evening's sequence of events and scuttled back upstairs, clasping the hot water bottle, which rolled around in his arms like a naughty baby. Once again, he crept under the duvet and pressed the bottle as close to himself as he could.

His mother had obviously been worrying about him as she was up extra early this morning and soon padded along to his room in her slippers and dressing gown.

She knocked gently on Eddie's door and entered the room

slowly, fearful of what she might discover. Her son was lying in bed, sweating and tossing and turning. His face was bright red and he was coughing and moaning in pain.

"Right, that is it," she said decisively. "I am going to call the doctor. You look awful."

She had to wait until the surgery opened at 8am before tele-phoning, but then her raised, anxious voice could be heard rico-cheting off the walls and bouncing upstairs to where Eddie was lying, thinking about how clever he had been and how it was all going according to plan.

CHAPTER 25

The doctor's room was small and cramped and Eddie's mum was sitting down firmly on the small chair next to the doctor's screen whilst her son stood next to her, pulling on his jumper after having been prodded and examined.

The doctor had listened to his chest, stared deep into his ears with a little light and asked him to "open wide" to inspect his throat. Eddie acted as sick as he possibly could, almost believing now that he really was suffering from a terrible illness. He had the inhaler buried deep in his trouser pocket, not knowing exactly how his plan might play out.

"Well, Eddie and mum," the doctor said firmly as he put his stethoscope away. "I can't really seem to find anything wrong with you, young man, that a few hours' sleep wouldn't cure. Go home and stay in bed for the day and I am sure that in a couple of days you will be as right as rain."

Eddie stared hopelessly at the elderly man in front of him. His glasses were pushed down his nose and he peered over the top of them at the patient in front of him and then glanced at the watch on his wrist. He was clearly in a hurry.

But his patient's mother was having none of it and her blunt directness played right into Eddie's hands.

"No, Doctor James, this isn't good enough," she said, leaning slightly towards him. "My boy is never ill. Never. If he says he is feeling bad, there is definitely something wrong with him. You need to give him antibiotics."

Eddie coughed as dramatically as he could, to remind the doctor just how bad he was.

"Miss Watson," answered Doctor James, sighing slightly and tapping on his computer to see whom his next patient was. "We do not give out antibiotics to anyone who asks for them. We have guidelines now, you know. There is a problem with bugs becoming resistant to them, which could mean in the future these medicines just wouldn't work on anyone. Imagine how awful that would be..."

Sitting back in her chair, her handbag planted on her lap and staring defiantly back at the doctor, Eddie's mother pursed her lips.

"I really don't care about all that," she said. "Eddie has never had antibiotics and he needs them now so you need to give them to him."

And then she added, for extra effect: "And we are going abroad in a couple of days so I can't have him really ill on holiday. I would make a complaint if that happened." Eddie was impressed with her quick-thinking. He knew she was lying.

The doctor turned to stare at her, not liking the threatening tone of her abrupt words. The two adults looked at eachother as Eddie stood, his heart beating in anxiety as he saw his plans begin to collapse around him.

Suddenly Doctor James breathed out deeply, as if he had decided it was easier to just give in, turned back to his computer and started tapping quickly.

"All right then," he mumbled. "I will prescribe some, but leave it a couple of days before you take them. See if Eddie gets better on his own first."

The printer scrambled into action and soon a green piece of paper was shooting out of it and was quickly grabbed by the doctor, who was clearly keen to get on to the next appointment. He picked up a pen and scribbled a signature on the bottom before handing it to Eddie's mum. She took it from him and gave him one of her beaming smiles before putting her hand around Eddie's shoulder and leading him out of the consulting room.

Eddie felt overjoyed. The first part of his plan had worked. Now he just needed to make sure the rest fell into place.

He needed to get into school and into the cupboard today to stand a chance of helping Charlotte. But how was he going to do that, having convinced his mother he was very ill? He was sure she would want him tucked up in bed.

He sat in the car on the way to the chemist to pick up his medicine, his hands tucked under him, desperately trying to work out just how he was going to get back into St Paul's and back into Charlotte's world. No Google searches were going to help him with that, he would just need a lot of cunning and a huge amount of luck.

CHAPTER 26

The paper bag containing the medicine was sitting on Eddie's lap as his mum drove the car back in the direction of their house. The sun was shining and she had music playing loudly on the car radio. Eddie could feel the minutes ticking away rapidly and he desperately tried to find a reason to stop off at the school on the way home.

"Mum," he said. "I need to get something from school on the way home."

"Oh no, babes. Don't worry about school today. You need to get better. We will go home and you can get tucked up in bed. Then I have to go to work. I have to be there in about half an hour. You will be OK on your own for a few hours, won't you?"

"Yes, I will be fine, but I need to pick up my homework. I can do it while you are at work." There was a note of desperation in his voice.

"No, you can stay in bed and get better," she said firmly.

"Please mum. I hate being in the house on my own and if I have my homework, it will give me something to do."

She looked over at him and her eyes narrowed. There was a flicker of guilt in her face, as if she knew she shouldn't really leave him on his own and wanted to make herself feel better about it.

"Well, you have changed," she muttered. "You have never been interested in school before. I suppose I should be pleased that you are finally bothered about homework. All right then, we will stop by the school and get it. But you will have to hurry or I will be late for work."

She pulled into a side street and turned the car around to head off to the school, humming along to the music from the radio. Eddie stuffed the paper bag with the medicine into his other pocket. It bulged out a bit, so he pulled his jumper down to hide it.

CHAPTER 27

Eddie and his mother stood outside the entrance to the school, ringing the buzzer to alert the office that someone was waiting.

He looked around, thinking how different it appeared now in comparison to the fields and trees which surrounded it in 1899. The white, plastic and glass which encased the proud date over the brick entrance looked so out of place and Eddie remembered how the playground had been filled with hoops and balls and children dressed in dull colours and white ribbons. They didn't have buzzers and high, metal fences in those days. Now, it seemed a bit like a prison rather than a children's school.

A buzzer told them they could open the door and go in. Eddie's mother went over to the glass window, which opened into the office and explained that Eddie was off sick, but needed to quickly collect some homework that he wanted to do.

Mrs Brown, the school secretary, raised her eyebrows a little and peered around Eddie's mum to look at her son. Eddie coughed a bit to prove that he was unwell. His face was no longer red and hot, as he hadn't had any help from his hot water bottle for a while now, so he made the cough sound as dramatic as he could.

"Doesn't he just want to stay in bed and get better?" said the secretary, turning back to the parent standing in front of her.

"Well, he is determined to do this work," answered Eddie's mum. "I don't want to discourage him."

"All right," said Mrs Brown, looking up at the clock. "It's nearly break time, so everyone is still in class. Nip down there quickly and get it. Mrs Jameson is there, so you can let her know."

She stood up and went over to the headteacher's door, which was on the other side of the office, to let him know.

Eddie didn't need telling twice. He walked quickly through the entrance hall and down through the corridor that led to his classroom. This was it, he thought, patting the bulge of the medicine on one side, and the inhaler on the other, to make sure they were both there.

The corridor loomed ahead, full of its usual coats and bags. Everything was the same jumble of organised confusion. He could see the door half way down and felt it pulling, dragging him towards it. The electric buzz was stronger than ever and he knew that it was now or never.

"Eddie Watson!"

A voice boomed down on him from behind. He turned quickly and saw Mr Evans standing a few paces behind him. His face was serious and angry. "I need to speak to you, NOW!"

He knows, thought Eddie. He knows I stole the inhaler. And then he just ran. He ran down the corridor, with the headteacher running behind him, trying to avoid abandoned bags lying on the floor.

Eddie was as quick as a bullet, but Mr Evans was even quicker. The boy grabbed the door and pulled it open just as Mr Evans reached him. His hand grasped Eddie's shoulder as he darted inside and tried to heave the door shut behind him, slipping his shoulder from Mr Evans. He felt a strength he had never experienced before fill his whole body as he pulled the door away from Mr Evans' grasp on the other side. It slammed shut.

Total blackness. Eddie felt the electricity from the handle buzz around his body as the frantic rattling on the other side of the door suddenly and completely stopped. All he could hear was his own ragged breathing and his blood pumping around like a beating drum. He had done it.

He stood in the darkness for a few moments to collect himself and calm down. The inhaler and the medicine were still in his pockets, he could feel them pressed against his legs. Now he just prayed that when he opened the door again he was where he hoped he would be – back in 1899.

The door opened a crack, squeaking slightly as Eddie pushed it. He put his eye to the crack, not wanting to see the furious face of his headteacher, Mr Evans, staring back at him. He held his breath as his eyes darted around the slither of view he had through the tiny gap.

Tiles. A high wooden ceiling. The sharp voice of a woman coming from the classroom in front of him. Childish voices chanting back. 1899. Thank God.

Eddie stepped out confidently as he was pretty sure that no one, apart from Charlotte, could see him in this other world. He plunged his hands into his pockets and felt the smooth plastic of the inhaler in one, and the crumpled bag of the tablets in the other. He was going to find her. And save her.

CHAPTER 28

Simmonds Bakery squatted in front of him, separated from the filthy, muddy road by a thin pavement. The windows were cloudy and Eddie could barely see inside when he peered through. He could just about make out the shape of a man moving around inside and a couple of customers waiting to be served.

He knew that when he went in, the door would open and people would wonder how, and why, it was being opened. This could be his chance, as the people inside were clearly busy and distracted.

Eddie opened the door a tiny bit, just enough to squeeze himself through, before shutting it quietly, hoping that no one had seen.

The man behind the counter, wearing a long, white apron splashed with patches of flour, was busily putting bread into a basket held up by a woman standing on the other side, in front of him.

"Here you are, Mrs Fellowes," said the man behind the counter. "That will be tuppence, please."

"Thank you, Mr Simmonds. There you are," said the woman, counting out a couple of pennies into the baker's hand. He turned around and placed the money into a box behind him.

The woman, wearing a heavy, brown dress covered by a shawl and a small brown hat on her head, gathered up her basket and walked right past Eddie to leave the shop. She looked right through him, but, strangely, stepped to one side as she got close to the boy standing almost in her path.

The door opened and shut behind her, leaving Mr Simmonds and his one other customer in the shop.

"Now then, Mrs Jones," he said, slightly wearily. "Let's see if that loaf you brought over to get baked is finally done."

The woman standing near the oven at the other end of the shop, looked up at him and nodded. He walked around the counter and over towards her and she turned to face the oven, which must have been radiating heat into the shop, although Eddie couldn't feel it.

He thought back to his confusion when he was last in the bakery. He now realised that the baker clearly charged people to bake loaves they had made at home. He wouldn't have to ask Charlotte after all. Maybe she wasn't even there to ask, he thought desperately, hoping beyond anything that he was in time to save her.

As the man and his customer were busy looking at the oven, Eddie grabbed his chance to slip into the house behind without them seeing. He ran around the counter and watched the two people carefully.

As the baker opened the heavy oven door, Eddie pulled the door behind the counter open, darted through, and closed it behind him with a small click. He waited for a moment, listening to hear if they would come and investigate why the door had opened and closed so strangely. But all he could hear was their muffled voices, discussing the loaf and how much payment was owed.

The corridor was just as it had been before. Nothing had changed. The brown wallpaper peeling in the same places and the stairs leading upwards on the right-hand side.

Eddie started to step up them, his fingers crossed that he wasn't too late and that Charlotte would still be upstairs. Or maybe, just maybe, she had got better. But he knew that she hadn't been in the classroom when he had briefly peered in after he had come out of the cupboard.

The door of her bedroom stood firmly closed in front of him and he put his head against it to listen. He could hear someone moving around inside, clattering and whispering. Maybe she was growing stronger and was just off school to allow her to recover. Then he heard her mother's voice.

"Here you are, my love," said the thin, worried voice through the door. "A bit of broth should make you feel better. Try to take a little. Sit up and I will spoon it into your mouth. You must try to eat something."

He heard the bedsprings creak as Mrs Simmonds clearly tried to raise Charlotte up so that she could feed her.

Then the coughing started. Agonising, weak coughs that went on and on until they faded away into tiny whimpers.

"Oh my love," Eddie heard through the door. "Just try a little bit. We must make you stronger."

He could stand it no longer and pushed the door open and stepped inside the room. Mrs Simmonds looked up, startled, from the bed at the door opening by itself. She stood up in confusion, and walked to the door, looking up and down the landing to see who had opened it.

Eddie was standing so close to her he could almost touch her, but something told him to hold back and that trying to touch someone in this world would not be a good idea. An invisible force made her lean away from the boy standing just to her side.

Charlotte was lying in the bed, exhausted. Her eyes were closed and her hair looked greasy and matted against the pillow. She was thinner than ever and a bowl of untouched, watery soup stood on the table next to the bed.

Her mother, clearly not understanding why the door had opened, walked gently back to her daughter and laid her palm lovingly on her forehead.

"What is to be done with you?" she asked, a sad and desperate look on her face. "I will leave you to sleep and come back to see you in an hour or so. I love you."

She kissed her daughter tenderly on the cheek, and left the room through the open door, closing it firmly behind her.

Eddie stood and watched his friend as she lay, helpless, on the bed. Her hands lay crossed over her chest, motionless. Every so often a little cough escaped from her and a wheezing sound echoed through the small room.

"Charlotte," he said, walking towards her. She did not open her eyes.

"Charlotte, look up," he said, a little louder, touching her cold hand on the bedcover. Her eyes fluttered open and she saw who it was. She managed a small smile.

"Lift me up gently," she said, her voice small and weak.

As Eddie helped pull her up to a sitting position, his friend slumped back onto her pillow. When he touched her, he felt the familiar sensation buzzing around his body. He was aware it was getting fainter now and worried that this was because Charlotte, herself, was fading away.

"How are you?" he asked, a little pointlessly bearing in mind what he could see in front of him.

"No better. Worse, if anything," she whispered. "There is nothing more that can be done."

"But there is, Charlotte," Eddie said, excitedly. "Look what I have brought you."

He reached into his pockets and pulled out the blue, plastic inhaler and the box of pills.

"These can save your life. I have brought them from my time to yours," continued Eddie, his voice shaking with hope.

Her frail fingers felt the smooth, cool plastic of the inhaler and she looked confused as she studied the cartridge in the end of it. She then opened the box and her hand stroked the stiff foil, which encased the rows of small, coated pills.

"But what are these?" It was an effort for her to even speak. "How can these things save me?"

"You need to trust me, Charlotte," pleaded Eddie. "I was given them by a doctor. This is called an inhaler."

He lifted up the blue inhaler and held it in front of her eyes.

"It's for people with asthma. And these," he waved the pills towards her. "These are called antibiotics. They weren't even discovered until 1928, but they are tiny miracles that can cure chest infections like you have."

Charlotte slumped back a little further and shook her head.

"I am sorry, Eddie. Thank you, but there is nothing you can do to help me now."

"But you MUST believe me. Antibiotics were discovered by a man called Alexander Fleming and we use them all the time in my world to cure all sorts of things."

She shut her eyes, trying to control her pain and her exhaustion. Eddie was frustrated. He had expected her to be overjoyed by what he had done and grab what he was offering. Her lack of enthusiasm shocked him. He realised she had given up, and decided, for the first time in his life, to lay himself bare and find out who he really was, what he had done, and why.

"Look, Charlotte. I am going to tell you why you have to take these pills," he began. She watched him carefully through her half-open eyes, listening with some interest to his words.

"I have always got into trouble at school and had sort of given up on it. I love my mum, but she is a bit of a pain. She never quite gets things sorted out and, although I know she loves me, she isn't that bothered about me doing well, so I couldn't really be bothered either.

"Since I met you, my life has changed, really changed. All I ever did was play on my computer and the internet."

Charlotte's face frowned as she didn't understand what he was talking about.

"I mean, my magic box. I have now seen there are lots of other things I can enjoy as well as the magic box. I have even made a couple friends at school called Alfie and Ethan, although I nearly blew it with Ethan when I pushed him over and he banged his head."

Charlotte gasped a little and muttered: "It was your friend that you pushed? How terrible!"

"Well, not on purpose, and he was OK in the end. But now, what I have just done… I don't know if he will ever forgive me if he finds out."

Eddie thought about Ethan's inhaler and how he had stolen it from the teacher's cupboard.

"OK? What does that word mean? And what have you done to this friend that he cannot forgive?"

"Oh, I don't know what the letters stand for, but it basically means he was all right," explained the boy, who was now gaining in confidence as he saw his friend hanging off his every word.

"Don't worry about what I have done, but I will be in bad trouble when I go back to my own time and my own school.

"And that is a bit sad because I am finally enjoying school a bit and I play football every break and I have even been round to Alfie's house for tea. That has never happened before. People just didn't want me around at my last school."

Charlotte looked at him in sympathy. She nodded her head silently and encouraged him to continue.

"When they find out what I have done, people will probably think I am bad and naughty and Ethan may never speak to me again. So you actually have to do this for my sake.

"I have used my magic box to find out what is wrong with you and what my world can do to help you. I have done some dangerous things to get this stuff and if you don't take it, everything I have done will have been a waste of time."

He looked intently at her, to make sure she was clear about what he was saying. Her eyes had softened and he could see she was interested.

"You can have a great future," Eddie pleaded. "Even though you are a girl. Do you know that in the future you will be able to vote and even become Prime Minister?"

A small laugh drifted from Charlotte, as she closed her eyes in disbelief.

"That is something I find difficult to believe," she said, her voice barely audible.

"We have a woman Prime Minister now!" said Eddie, excitedly. "She is called Tessa May. Well, I think that's her name," he added, thinking he was not absolutely sure of his facts.

"What about being a doctor? Could a girl do that, do you

think?" asked the girl gently, now staring directly at him.

"Oh yes, there are loads of women doctors," Eddie said enthusiastically. "Millions of them."

Charlotte was clearly thinking about this future, taking his words in.

He fell silent. He couldn't think of any more to say. He hoped he had done enough, and his eyes wandered around the room, with its fire crackling away in the grate, thinking about how different it was from his room at home. It was simple and uncomplicated, far away from the buzz of his computer and all the electronics that had crowded his head every evening. But also, far away from the medical help that everyone in his world took for granted.

"OK," she said, repeating the word he had said earlier.

She even managed to laugh a little as she said: "I trust you. I will take this special medicine and hope that it will make me better. And then maybe, in the future, I can have what you speak of. I could even become a doctor myself. That would be my dream."

Eddie clasped her hand and squeezed it happily, agreeing with her hopes for her future life, the tingling buzzing up and down his arms like tiny spiders.

He then explained how to take the pills and what to do with the inhaler. He helped her swallow the first pill and showed her how to breathe in the spray from the inhaler.

Immediately her breathing seemed clearer and less wheezy. Then, she directed him to the chest in the corner where there was a small, black box. He picked it out and took it over to her. Charlotte whispered that she was going to leave the inhaler and pills in the box in the drawer of her bedside table so that her mother didn't see them. Goodness knows what she would think of it all. It was better that she simply didn't know.

"Do you think you will come back, Eddie?" asked Charlotte, who was now very tired from all that Eddie had made her do. "Will I ever see you again?"

"I don't know," he said truthfully. "All I know is that the door only works when I feel that strong electricity pulling me towards it. There were a couple of weeks when it didn't do that at all. It doesn't seem to be in my control." He thought about the hourglass on the door's handle with its sand seeping time away.

The light in the room fell onto her tired face, but she made an effort to hold his hand and squeeze it.

"Even if this doesn't work," she said. "I know what you have done for me and you are a truly great friend. You are the kindest boy I have ever met."

Her voice drifted away as she fell into a deep sleep. Eddie hoped it was the sleep of recovery and that her body was beginning to be mended by the gifts he had brought.

It was time to leave and face what was waiting for him back at school.

He knew that Mr Evans was waiting on the other side of the door and that his mum was standing in the school office.

Charlotte had said he was the kindest boy she had ever met, but, as far as the school was concerned, he was a nasty, rotten thief.

CHAPTER 29

The door was there in front of him, silently marking the path back into his own time. He stood facing it in the darkness, waiting for the inevitable. Like a hammer smashing down with sudden force, the handle started rattling loudly and he could hear Mr Evans' angry voice crash through the wood.

"Eddie Watson, come out now. Stop holding on to the handle and step outside this instant."

The rattling started again and the handle turned swiftly, allowing light to flood the cupboard, revealing its stored boxes and bits of wood. Mr Evans almost fell into the room on top of Eddie and just managed to hold onto the side of the doorway to steady himself.

He looked down at his pupil with real fury in his eyes.

"You need to come with me, young man, and explain yourself," said the headteacher.

He then stepped across to the classroom door and opened it. Mrs Jameson looked up in surprise from where she was sitting next to Ethan, helping him with his work.

"Mrs Jameson, please ask your teaching assistant to take the class for a few moments. I need you to come to my office," Mr Evans announced firmly, before closing the door.

Eddie glanced down at the handle and saw there were only a few grains of sand hesitating on the edge of the top part of the hourglass. Maybe time's running out for Eddie Watson, he thought sadly.

Mr Evans turned back to his pupil, put his hand firmly on Eddie's shoulder and marched him down the corridor towards the school's reception area.

Eddie could see his mother standing in the office, chatting away to Mrs Brown, completely unaware of what was coming next. He felt sorry that she was going to be disappointed in him, but knew that if he told anyone the truth, they simply would not believe it.

Before, when Eddie had been in trouble at school, he had become very angry and had tried to blame everyone else for his problems. It was always someone else's fault, never his. But this time was different.

He felt very calm as he was asked to sit down in Mr Evans' office, and looked away when Mrs Jameson came in and viewed him with a questioning, solemn expression. He had taken the inhaler and he was not going to deny it.

His mother appeared confused as they asked her to step in too, saying they had something "serious" to discuss with her. Her shoulders slumped as she understood that Eddie's run of good behaviour had now run out.

The teachers knew he was the thief, it could only have been him, and there was simply no one else to blame this time.

CHAPTER 30

"Suspended," yelled his mother, the words spitting out in fury. "And I have had to call work and tell them I couldn't come in today because of that stupid meeting at school. They might sack me now and where will we be then? And you PROMISED me, Eddie. You promised that you would try at this school. I don't know why I even listened to you.

"Why did you take that stupid inhaler? You haven't even managed to explain why. Ethan is supposed to be your friend and you took his inhaler for no reason and you can't tell anyone what you have done with it.

"I don't understand you Eddie. I don't know how much more of this I can take. I am not sure you are even ill – you certainly seem much better all of a sudden. Was all that coughing and stuff so you could be off school and avoid getting into trouble? And where is the medicine? You can't even tell me where you put the antibiotics? You are incredible!"

They were sitting in the kitchen, unwashed plates and saucepans surrounding them like a silent audience. Eddie picked at a few of the crumbs on the table in front of him, hardly daring to look up and meet his mother's eyes.

"I'm sorry," he said quietly, thinking that there was no point trying to justify what he had done.

"Well, go up to your room and think about what you have

done. I am so ashamed of you," his mother said, stifling a sob.

Eddie slouched upstairs and sat on his bed. His mum was ashamed of him, yet he knew he had been brave and kind. Kindness that he couldn't tell a single person about, except Charlotte. She was the only one who knew the truth.

He went over to his computer and sat sadly in front of it. Mr Evans had suspended him for one day and told him that when he returned, he was expected to "toe the line" or worse would follow. Mrs Jameson had looked at him with concern, wondering what had made him do such a terrible thing.

"Just imagine, Eddie," she had said, "if Ethan had suffered an asthma attack at school and his inhaler hadn't been here for him. Just think how awful that would have been."

That possibility had never crossed his mind.

He walked over to his desk and turned on the computer. Games and Youtube videos certainly did not appeal to him just now. He absent-mindedly turned on the machine, not really knowing what to do with it. Maybe he could watch a film to take his mind off the horrible telling-off he had been given.

The excitement of telling Charlotte about the medicine he had managed to get her was fading. She seemed a long, long way away and he wondered if he would ever see her again or learn if she had recovered.

His hands hovered over the keyboard and his mind wandered to the museum competition. He had never spoken to Charlotte about it, as she had been too unwell. His mind drifted back to Mrs Jameson telling the class about the competition and how their work would be printed onto a board and how the winner would get £100.

All of a sudden, he found himself opening a Word document.

"I can do this," he thought. "I can write this myself and show the school that I am not hopeless and stupid. I don't need Charlotte to help me."

For the next two hours, his hands flew over the letters, tapping and appearing on his screen in sentences which told the story of a young girl, desperate to learn in Victorian times.

About a school with strict teachers who caned their children for not understanding simple lessons. About girls who dreamed of a future in which they could play an equal part and become doctors, lawyers or even Prime Ministers. About children who wore caps and collars and white ribbons in their hair whilst playing simple games in the fresh air, surrounded by trees and open fields. Children who had no computers, *Crash or Dash* or Trickster to distract them from reality. It was almost as if Charlotte was standing behind him with her quiet energy and determination, willing him on, encouraging him to try harder. Believing in him.

At last he was finished and he read his work through several times to correct full stops and spelling mistakes.

It was the most he had ever written and as he read it through, he felt a glow of satisfaction spread through him. This is good, he told himself. Really good.

CHAPTER 31

Eddie was nervous about going back to school the next day. He knew that his friendship with Ethan was bound to suffer after he discovered that it was Eddie who had taken the inhaler. He felt sad about that, as he had enjoyed the lunchtime games with the boys and had even been thinking about joining them on the local playing field in the evenings for a knockabout.

After a quick talk with Mr Evans and his mum to discuss the "terms for his return to school", Eddie walked dejectedly down to the classroom.

He was a little late as the discussion had lasted until after the bell had been rung and he had to hang his coat and bag up in the deserted corridor. The children in his class were busily getting ready for the day behind the closed door of the classroom. Eddie peered up into the room through the windows from the corridor, remembering the strict teacher tapping on the board as the cold, shivering children repeated phrases after her.

He went quietly into the classroom, hardly glancing at the brown door, and hoping that no one would notice him. He always seemed to be hoping that no one would notice him.

"Hi Eddie. Late again!" said Ethan, smiling broadly, his museum competition writing in his hand. "Are you better?"

Eddie stared at him in confusion. Why was he being so nice?

"Er, yes, I am, thanks," he replied. "What did they say about me being off yesterday?"

Ethan carried on straightening the books on his desk and flicking through the messy, crumpled pages of writing in his hand.

"I think they said you had a cold or something," he answered, not really interested in Eddie's state of health. "I hope you are up to footie at lunchtime as the Year 4s think they are going to beat us. They are mad!"

"How are you?" asked Eddie, cautiously. "Any asthma attacks yesterday?" The question must have seemed a bit odd, but Ethan didn't react.

"Nope. I haven't had one for ages, to be honest. It's funny you should ask, because my inhaler went missing the day before yesterday. No one knows what happened to it and my mum thinks Mrs Jameson just lost it.

"Anyway, mum was pretty fed up as she had to go to the doctor's and get another one last night. She was cross as she said she had loads to do. She has always got loads to do according to her!"

So, the school had not told Ethan that Eddie had taken the inhaler. He felt a wave of gratitude flow over him as he knew his friendship with Ethan and Alfie had not been ruined. He looked over at Mrs Jameson and smiled weakly. She smiled back and came over.

"Feeling better?"

"Yes. And thank you, Mrs Jameson," answered Eddie, hoping that she understood what he was thanking her for.

"I hope that you can concentrate now on school work and doing your best," she said, a note of warning in her voice. "Now that your 'cough' is better."

"Yes, I will try," answered her pupil, looking down at the desk.

At lunchtime, Eddie stayed behind in the classroom to speak to his teacher. He didn't mention anything about the inhaler or his suspension the day before, but told her he had written his entry to the museum competition, adding that he had done it on his computer and didn't have a printer.

"Get your mother to email it to my school address and I will print it off for you," the teacher said, as she sat down with a pile of maths books to mark in front of her. She jotted down the email address on a scrap of paper and handed it to him.

"I am really looking forward to seeing it, and well done for making the effort. You are an intelligent boy, Eddie, and I am sure if you try hard, you can succeed at this school."

Maybe I am and maybe I will, thought Eddie.

CHAPTER 32

L ife was getter better. Eddie had started going over to the park to play with his friends after school, instead of hiding out in his bedroom to obsess over computer games or his favourite Youtubers.

He felt his head was clearer and he felt angry less often. Even if someone tackled him a bit roughly, or scored a goal that shouldn't have been allowed, he managed to control his temper and let it go.

Sometimes he remembered what he had done to Liam at his old school and felt a little guilty, but the fresh air and rough and tumble of the kickabouts soon blew away his bad thoughts. He was starting to look forward, rather than thinking about how bad his life was in comparison to other people's.

In class, Mrs Jameson had printed off the work he had written for the museum competition, which he had managed (with some difficulty) to persuade his mum to email to her. His teacher had stood in front of him, holding his precious work and looking at him in astonishment.

"You wrote this?" she had said, with disbelief.

"Yes," answered Eddie, embarrassed but proud at the same time. "The day I was suspended. I didn't have anything else to do, so I just decided to get on with it."

"It is incredible," stuttered his teacher. "I must show it to Mr Evans. He won't believe it. It's full of so much detail about Victorian schools and children. How did you manage to find all this out?"

"Er, I … researched it on the internet," said Eddie, looking down and tapping the leg of the table with his shoe. "I like looking stuff up on the internet."

Eddie then remembered he had one more question to ask his teacher, who had now walked back to her desk to sit down and sort the papers scattered on it in untidy piles.

"Mrs Jameson," said the boy, pulling his sleeves down over his knuckles. "Can I ask you something else?"

She sat back in her chair and turned towards him, giving him her full attention.

"St Paul's is a Victorian school, isn't it?"

"Oh yes. It was built in 1882 – it says so over the front door. It has a long and interesting history I believe."

"You know the school bell?" She nodded. "Is that Victorian too?"

"I think it is, yes. Mr Evans is always keen to look after it carefully as it is so old. Maybe we shouldn't still be ringing it, but he thinks it should be used as it is part of the school's past. I agree with him. Just think of all the children who have heard that ringing and who have followed it into class. It sends a tingle up my spine!"

And Eddie thought back to all those children in long dresses, caps and leather boots, who were called into class by that bell more than a hundred years ago as he stood and watched, invisible to all. Well, nearly all.

However, the door of the cupboard in the corridor remained firmly silent.

There was no magnetic pull, no static and no adventurous journeys into another age. At times, when he passed it while going to get his trainers or something from his bag, Eddie ran his hand over the handle. Nothing. He looked sadly at the chips in the wood and felt the cool metal of the handle and saw that the sand in the hourglass had not moved. The memory of Charlotte carefully using the inhaler and reading the instructions on the box of medicine was now hazy and foggy in his mind.

He told himself, once again, that it could all have been a strange dream, or his imagination playing tricks on him. It was possible that Charlotte had never existed and he had simply stolen the inhaler for no reason. Perhaps he had dropped it somewhere and simply forgotten. He had no idea. And finding proof of what had happened was simply impossible: if she had existed at all, she was now beyond his reach.

Eddie decided to enjoy the present. He played outside, he had fun with his friends and he even started to read *Harry Potter and the Goblet of Fire* and discovered he enjoyed reading almost as much as he now enjoyed writing.

One day as he passed the door, his eyes were drawn to the hourglass pattern carved into the handle.

Children walked busily past him as he pretended to fiddle with his bag whilst really studying the symbol. He realised with shock that the sand had nearly all trickled through. There were only a few grains left in the top part of the timer.

And then an event happened which changed Eddie's life for ever.

CHAPTER 33

T he class filed into a special morning assembly, being told to "sit down quietly" by Mr Evans, who was standing at the front of the hall.

None of the children knew what the assembly was about, as the teachers had not told them.

Eddie was sitting between Alfie and Ethan, which Mrs Jameson didn't usually allow as they tended to chat a little when they weren't supposed to. But she had seemed a little distracted, and the boys had managed to slip into formation and slope their way into the hall together without her realising. They sat poking and pinching eachother, quietly sniggering and avoiding the attention of the teachers sitting around the hall.

Mrs Jameson walked to the front and whispered quietly to the headteacher, who nodded and scanned his eyes solemnly over the Year 5 children. His stare rested on Eddie and he turned back to the teacher and they whispered again.

Eddie couldn't help but notice their quiet conversation and he felt a tremor of panic, just like the old days. He desperately tried to work out what he had done. Why had they called the whole school into this assembly? He went back over the last week and thought about what he could possibly be blamed for. He was sure he had done everything they had asked of him, but here he was, once again, being whispered about and singled out as the bad person.

Counting slowly, he tried to slow down his pounding heart

as he argued with himself that surely he had done nothing naughty. He couldn't bear his mother to tell him again how ashamed she was of him... and just when life was improving.

Mr Evans cleared his throat. The children all looked up at him expectantly.

"Well, children," he said, Mrs Jameson still standing by his side. "I have a very important announcement."

Eddie looked down at his shoes as he could tell that Mrs Jameson was trying her hardest NOT to look at him. He knew she was looking everywhere except in his direction. His hands were clasped together and he felt hot and uncomfortable.

"We have a very special visitor waiting outside who is coming to make an announcement about one of our children," continued the headteacher, in a serious and clear voice.

As he finished, the hall doors opened and a woman, smartly dressed in a suit and holding a brown envelope, entered the hall. She was wearing glasses and had her hair tied up in a ponytail. And she was followed into the hall by ... Eddie's mum.

Ethan and Alfie dug Eddie in the ribs and turned to him questioningly.

"What's your mum doing up there?" whispered Ethan, so confused he wasn't bothered about getting into trouble for talking.

"I have no idea," said Eddie, glaring at his mum and feeling furious with her for not warning him. He couldn't believe she would agree to be part of his humiliation. He felt the old flames of anger flicker through him and struggled to control himself. His teachers were bad enough, but his *mum*?

"I would like to introduce you to Miss Downing," said Mr Evans.

But Eddie hardly heard what he was saying as his head started to swim and his thoughts scrambled to make sense of what was happening.

The lady started speaking and the children sat, entranced by her words. His mother stood by the door, looking at Eddie and smiling. Why was she smiling, thought Eddie? He heard nothing the suit lady said as the pounding in his head got louder and louder.

And as Miss Downing finished, the whole school turned to stare at Eddie. Every child in the school was focused on him and all the teachers were looking at him too. Hundreds of eyes, looking and staring. Eddie glanced around anxiously, not knowing what to do.

"Eddie Watson," said Mr Evans, his face breaking into a beaming smile. "Please come up to the front of the hall. After all, you have just won first prize in the museum writing competition."

Alfie and Ethan were both staring at Eddie, their mouths hanging open in surprise.

"Oh my God," said Alfie, not worrying now at all about being told off. "You have won FIRST PRIZE. Go on, you need to go up to the front."

As if in a dream, his legs wobbling and his hands shaking, Eddie staggered to the front of the hall. He could see his mother coming towards him with a huge grin on her face and the lady in the suit smiling encouragingly at him.

He stood between his headteacher and Miss Downing, his mother behind him squeezing his shoulders in delight. Then the whole school erupted into an avalanche of cheering and clapping.

And Eddie's mother leaned over to whisper in his ear: "Eddie, I am so proud of you."

CHAPTER 34

The morning passed by in a dream-like haze. Eddie would remember that day for the rest of his life. He was congratulated by everyone: Mr Evans, Mrs Jameson, Miss Downing, his friends and children from all the other classes.

Everyone wanted to know him and tell him how well he had done. His heart felt like it would burst with pride. Even the local newspaper turned up to take a photo with him, Miss Downing and Mr Evans. Eddie's mum even managed to get in on the act as she insisted she needed to be in the photo "with my son" too.

"Well, Eddie," said Miss Downing, as they sat in the head-teacher's office, sipping on tea and eating biscuits. Eddie thought for a brief moment how different this was to the last time he had sat in that office, when Mr Evans had warned him to 'toe the line'.

"You know what the prize will be don't you? Your work will be printed on to a large board and will be part of our museum exhibition on the lives of young people in the past. And not only that, you also get a lovely £100! We were so impressed by your writing. It was almost as if you had been there and experienced it yourself!"

Eddie thought to himself that she didn't know how close to the truth her words actually were.

He was the centre of everyone's attention for doing something good and he found he was really enjoying it. Basking in the praise Miss Downing was giving him, Eddie smiled gratefully at her.

"And so, we want you to come to the museum and see your work in pride of place. The exhibition has all been organised and we are just waiting for the board with your writing on to arrive.

"So we have arranged for a grand opening next Wednesday at 2pm and you will be our guest of honour. I think even the Mayor is coming!"

Eddie felt like a superstar. He also knew that there was one person with whom he would have loved to share his triumph.

CHAPTER 35

It was nearly time to go home when Eddie needed to nip out to the toilet. He grabbed a toilet pass and jogged down the corridor to the boys'. When he had finished, he sauntered up towards his classroom, avoiding the usual debris scattered over the floor. The brown door sat silently staring at him and he reached out towards it to remember the adventures he had experienced.

A bright blue spark crackled from the handle into his fingers. The strongest and most dramatic flash yet. He felt its tremors shoot through his body and knew what he had to do. There was no time to think and consider. The stories of time were pulling him back into the past, and he was not going to resist seeing her again.

He quickly hung the toilet pass over his peg, knowing that any journey would only last a couple of seconds in his own time, and grabbed the handle, which almost stuck to his hand with a magnetic pull. Glancing down at the handle, Eddie could see just a tiny grain of sand hovering on the edge, waiting to tip itself finally into the glass below. Suddenly he knew what it meant. Time was nearly up. This would be his last chance to see Charlotte again. If she still lived.

Throwing the door open, he dashed inside and pulled it back to shut it.

The darkness covered him completely and the boy stood for a few moments, hoping that he would not be disappointed.

And as he carefully creaked the door open, he almost shouted for joy as he saw the dusty tiles on the floor and the ceiling soaring up above him. He had done it. He was back! Now he just had to find her.

The classroom in front of him was empty except for the stern-looking teacher writing on the board with chalk, peering over her glasses as she copied from a book she was holding in her hand. She looked up briefly as if she had heard something, but soon returned to her writing.

Children's voices could be heard outside and Eddie realized it must be break time and that they were probably absorbed in their hoops and balls on the playground. He walked to the end of the corridor and opened the door, knowing that now he knew his way around this school which was so similar yet so changed from his own.

The sun was shining brightly and the trees were covered in thick, green leaves. Eddie quickly calculated it had been about a month since he had last been through the door. Three weeks at least. That would mean in this other time zone it would be months ahead. It must be summer time and nearly the end of the school year.

The playground was full of children running around, their clothes lighter than they had been in the winter months when Eddie had been before.

He was braver this time, knowing that none of them would see him. He wandered through their games, but hoops swerved around him and the children seemed to have some sixth sense which meant they never touched him.

Girls and boys shot about, enjoying the sunshine and their brief break away from that strict, suffocating classroom. He scanned desperately around, trying to spot Charlotte, but all he could see was a mass of children running, laughing and jumping.

Then, in the midst of all the youthful action, a thin figure stood still, the others still charging around her like little planets circling the sun. She stood silently and stared directly at him with her seeing eyes.

She walked straight over, a broad smile on her face and a touch of colour in her cheeks. The girl stood in front of him and couldn't help herself laughing out loud with joy.

It was Charlotte. She had survived.

CHAPTER 36

The two children looked around them, not wanting to attract attention by anyone noticing Charlotte standing and speaking to thin air.

"I cannot believe that you are here. This is my greatest wish come true," whispered Charlotte. "Come on, let's go over to the oak tree."

Eddie could not speak, he was so relieved to see her there, breathing and alive. He trotted after her to sit on the other side of the oak tree, a tree which still reigned proudly over his own playground in his own time. They sat down on the bark and dry mud by the tree.

"So what happened?" said Eddie.

"I took your medicine," said Charlotte, staring at his face and still smiling broadly. "And very soon I started to feel better. I had to hide it from mother and father, which was difficult, but they never suspected a thing. I still have a cough, but that is the asthma. I used that blue machine when it got really bad. It has run out but it is now summer and I am always better in the summer."

She suddenly looked serious and fiddled with a piece of bark with her fingers.

"You saved my life, Eddie," she whispered, and he saw her eyes were full of tears. "And I will always be grateful to you. Did you get into trouble for what you did? You never told me what you had done that was so bad and dangerous. I hope you didn't get the cane for my sake."

Eddie laughed: "Oh we don't have the cane in my time, remember. I just got suspended, that is I had to stay at home for a day."

Charlotte nodded: "Ah yes, your strange punishments in the future. This future sounds both wonderful and peculiar at the same time.

"I have decided," she added firmly. "That I owe my life to this medicine from your time and that I believe you when you say that ladies are able to have professions and make their own choices. I am going to work hard and be one of those women, maybe even a doctor. I am determined."

Eddie nodded vigorously. He told her all the different jobs that women do in his time, from engineering to teaching, from being a lawyer to being surgeons. He didn't talk about robots or airline pilots as he thought that she probably would start to doubt that he was telling the truth.

"And what about you, Eddie? What are you going to do with your life? Are you still practising on your magic box?"

He thought about his computer and his obsession with gaming.

"The magic box is good for some things," he said. "But playing football and reading books is great too. And I have discovered I really like writing."

He then told her all about the museum competition and how he had used their adventures to describe what life was like in her time and had won the first prize. Charlotte clapped her hands with delight.

"Eddie, you are a famous writer," she said, coughing a little in her excitement and placing a hand on her chest as she winced.

They sat together for a moment in silence, both thinking about their future and what it could hold for them. Charlotte a doctor and Eddie... well he wasn't sure yet.

"But I have to ask you," asked Eddie, suddenly. "Are you real? Is all this real or am I just dreaming. I can't work it out. It all seems real when I am here, but when I go back to my own time it seems distant and hazy. I keep asking myself if I have made it all up."

Charlotte turned to face him and smiled. She took hold of his hand and held it tight. There was no strange electricity now. It seemed to have died away and Eddie's head was as clear as the sunshine which streamed down on him.

"Feel this hand, Eddie," she said. "I am as real as you are."

But he knew that once he returned to his modern day school, he would begin to doubt it. Eddie started nibbling his fingers, wondering how he could prove to himself that this had happened and she had really existed. With a flash of inspiration, he grabbed her other hand.

"I know, Charlotte. Have you still got the inhaler and the box of medicine?" he gasped, desperate to hear that she had.

"Yes, I have kept them in my box next to my bed. My mother never looks in there as she knows it is where I keep my special, private things," she replied.

"Why don't we bury them? Here, under the oak tree? Then when I go back to my time, I can dig them up and I will know that this has all been true."

Eddie then told her about how the handkerchief had collapsed into dust in the cupboard when he had grabbed it from her hand by mistake. They both knew it would be impossible to take anything that had been in Charlotte's time back to his own. It would simply turn to dust. They suddenly became serious and quiet as they realised that Charlotte had been lucky to not suffer the same fate when she tried to go into Eddie's time. Burying the evidence was the only possible answer.

The sunlight flickered down through the trees as the school bell sounded through the soft air. The children were being called back to class, to be drilled on repeating phrases, and creating beautiful lines of handwriting. Eddie knew now that this same bell called children to class in his own time. It made him smile.

Charlotte stood up slowly.

"But I don't have them here. I will have to return after school.

Can you wait for me?"

"Yes, I will wait. I will wait right here until you come back, but remember to bring a box with you, one that will last for more than a hundred years."

With one last smile and one last wave, Charlotte went off to join her friends for her afternoon lessons.

Eddie lay and dozed in the shade of the afternoon sun, waiting for her to return and for him to be able to prove that she was a real, living person and that he was not dreaming.

CHAPTER 37

E ddie woke with a start when he felt a hand shake his shoulder gently. Charlotte was there in front of him, quite pale now and obviously tired after her day. She was holding a metal box and opened it to reveal the inhaler and box with the foil sheet which had held the life-saving pills.

"I have to hurry," she said, breathlessly. "I have had to sneak out and my parents will wonder where I am soon. I shouldn't be here and if I get caught, I will be in trouble with the school. Let's bury this quickly.

"But just in case we don't see eachother again, I want to tell you, Eddie, I will never forget you until the day I die. Even if I live to be a famous doctor and a hundred years old!"

The two children stared at eachother and then down at the metal box. Then they gave eachother a hug and stepped back, both with tears in their eyes. Charlotte hid the box under her smock in case someone should come along.

And so the pair of children, one with a long, white smock hanging to almost her ankles and the other with knee-length, grey shorts and a bright red jumper, huddled over a patch in the soil. They looked around themselves and whispered anxiously.

The boy sat back on his black leather shoes and looked up at the oak tree, which loomed over them. The girl, grimacing as she coughed quietly, turned her head to see what he was looking at and nodded quickly before tapping at the soil with a flat stone. The boy then leant forward and their heads almost touched as they quickly dug into the black, stony earth. Soil flew up around them in little puffs as they worked away, one of them glancing behind them every few seconds as if fearful of something – or someone.

Eventually they created a little hole in the soil deep enough to satisfy their mysterious, secret mission. As they both rapidly scanned around them one last time, the girl pulled, from under her smock, the silver metal box. She rattled it gently at the boy and he allowed a smile to pass across his face. Carefully, he took it from her hands and pushed it deep into the earth before they both scooped up the soil that was scattered around them and pressed it over the top of the little hill, pushing the blackness down hard on top of the metal box.

When they finished, there was just a tiny mound to betray their efforts. They took it in turns to stamp hard on it – her with her brown, battered boots and he with his shiny black shoes which were now speckled with earth. They scuttled about, grabbing small stones to sprinkle on top of the bare earth, and soon it looked as if no one had ever disturbed the flattened ground.

They stood and faced each other and the girl coughed again, holding her hand to her chest as if in pain. He touched her arm as tiny beads of sweat broke out on her skin. She was thin and quite pale, although a tint of pink flushed across her cheeks. He looked at her through his long, dark fringe, which skimmed low over his eyes. They both looked up together now into the green leaves of the oak tree, which were dancing lightly in the breeze as if rustling a message across the stories of time.

The boy and the girl both smiled as if pleased with themselves and briefly held hands before turning and walking briskly away in opposite directions.

Eddie looked back and saw Charlotte walking away down the street, disappearing into the distance of time.

CHAPTER 38

That night, Eddie lay in bed thinking about the momentous events that had happened earlier that day. He glowed with pleasure over his success in the museum writing competition and allowed himself to remember how his mum had held his shoulders and told him how proud she was.

The adventures with Charlotte seemed slightly dimmed and distant and he almost struggled to remember each detail. She seemed a lifetime away, and he once again wondered if she was real or part of his imagination.

But he knew, now, that he had a way of proving to himself whether she existed or not. Tomorrow he would go and dig under the tree and see if the metal box was there. He had a sad suspicion that he would find nothing.

Everything was back to normal at school the following day. There was a morning of maths and English and he felt that his teacher, Mrs Jameson, treated him with a new respect, as if she believed in him and knew that he was capable of doing well. He was even chosen to read out his story at the end of the English lesson and the others listened in silence to their now-prizewinning writer. The words on the page creating their own world and stories were a joy to him now, and Eddie started to believe that he could really write. Charlotte had told him he was famous; in a way, he actually was.

When he had arrived at school that morning and hung up

his bag on his peg, Eddie had sneaked a glance at the door and its silver handle. The hourglass pattern had disappeared. There was no sand trickling through and no stars and swirls. When he leant closer, he could see there were still lines and scratches, but they looked like the result of years of people rushing past, hands turning the knob and the haphazard dents of time. He knew the magic had gone for good. He just hoped that his plan for later would prove to him once and for all that it had ever existed at all.

At lunchtime, the boys all gathered to grab their trainers ready for another battle with the Year 4s. This was a friendly but deadly contest that went on day after day, week after week, and was a constant source of bitterness and joy – depending on who was triumphant at the end of the playtime.

Everyone wanted Eddie to play as he had proved he was skilled and capable on the pitch. But he knew that he had something more important to do, and something that he needed to do all on his own.

"I'm not feeling too great," he explained to Alfie and Ethan. "I think I will take a break from football today."

"Oh, you can't," whined Ethan, running his hands through his red hair. "We need you. You have to play. Thomas from Year 4 will mark me if you're not there and he is such a pain."

Alfie joined in: "Don't be a spoilsport. You were all right this morning. What's wrong with you?"

"Dunno," mumbled Eddie, trying to sound a little under the weather. After all, he had already had some practice at pretending to be ill. "I feel a bit sick. I will be fine later, I'm sure."

The boys gave up and went off to their daily battle, muttering about how Thomas "cheated all the time" and how he "can't take losing". Eddie watched them disappear up the corridor towards the playground.

He grabbed his coat and a metal spoon he had taken from the kitchen drawer before he left for school that morning.

The oak tree was set apart a little from the main playground, in the wooded area. There were often lots of children playing around there at lunchtime, so he had to be careful to avoid being seen.

Eddie remembered that he and Charlotte had dug the box on the other side of the tree, away from where the children played, so he hoped he could dig without anyone noticing.

The oak tree stood proudly where it had also stood more than one hundred years earlier. It was still holding on to its leaves, despite the grip of late autumn, which dragged the leaves from branches and discarded them into the wind. It was a chilly, but bright, day and Eddie looked about to make sure that no one spotted him behaving strangely.

He edged to the back of the tree and then slipped behind it. The ground was flat but not that hard as it had rained a couple of days before, softening the mud and making it possible to dig into it with his spoon.

Looking up into the branches, Eddie tried to judge exactly where they had buried the metal box. He knelt down and started to scoop the earth away, looking up every couple of seconds to see if anyone had spotted him. All the children were focused on the wooden play equipment, and no one noticed the boy busily burrowing into the earth.

Scoop after scoop of soil flew up in little bursts as Eddie scurried away at his task. How deep did he need to go, he wondered? He tried three different spots and there was no sign of any metal, no clinking of the spoon against something hard.

The effort of digging and watching was beginning to tire him and his breathing became harder and beads of sweat broke out on his brow.

Eddie sat back on his knees, looking sadly at the piles of soil he had created. It was hopeless. Well, at least he now knew that Charlotte had not really existed and that he must just be a little bit bonkers. Or maybe he just had a super-active imagination that made things he thought about seem real. But then, he questioned, how had he known all those details about what school was like in those days and what the children had worn?

In frustration, he jabbed the spoon into the earth on the side of the third hole he had made. Then he heard it and felt it. The clang of metal. A hard surface under the edge of the spoon.

He frantically leant forward and dug furiously, hardly aware of anyone or anything around him. Hands working quickly, he started to uncover a silver lid which seemed to rise up from the darkness of the soil, like a fish swimming to the surface. His fingers shaking, he scrambled at the soil to uncover it.

Finally it was revealed. A metal box, dented and dirty, but like a beautiful gift wrapped in a thousand wishes.

Eddie pulled it from its hiding place and slowly opened the lid. Inside was the inhaler, the blue colour faded into a pale shimmer, and bits of decayed card which covered a silver foil which had once contained lines of pills.

"So," breathed Eddie, laughing and leaning back on his heels. "You are real, after all."

He grabbed the box and buried it in the secrecy of his coat, hugging it close to his heart.

CHAPTER 39

Eddie sat in his bedroom with the metal box on his lap. He stared at it, his hand gently lying on its aged, rusted surface. It was incredible, really, how well it had survived the test of time. The plastic shell of the inhaler looked almost as if it had been made yesterday, and only its faded colour was a clue to how long it had been buried. The boy imagined it lying there, under the soil, for all those years. All the feet that had charged around on top of it with no idea of the time capsule that was hiding underneath.

He now knew that Charlotte Simmonds was a real person and that, somehow, he had managed to go against all the laws of science and travel back in time to see her. This metal box and its contents proved beyond doubt that what Eddie had suspected was a dream, was in fact a reality.

Their last proper conversation played again in Eddie's mind. How Charlotte had been inspired by his talk of a future in which she could play an important part, in which girls were not second class citizens and were equal to boys.

Eddie had never really thought about this before. He had always found girls annoying and full of themselves. Now he started to see them differently. Charlotte had walked off, brimming with determination to make something of her life, despite the hurdles in front of her.

His eyes wandered over to his computer. He had a sudden thought, which sent goosebumps prickling over his skin. His fingers typed into his favourite Google search engine and the familiar box appeared on the screen.

He keyed in the words: Charlotte Simmonds.

A whole load of Charlotte Simmonds appeared in front of him, linking him to facebook pages and twitter accounts. These people lived all over the world and their pictures smiled back at him with their young faces and modern clothes. None of them was his Charlotte.

Her words echoed in his head: "I will never forget you, Eddie, until the day I die. Even if I live to be a hundred years old!"

A hundred years old, he thought. Absent-mindedly, he calculated when that would have been. Thinking back to their conversations and what she had told him about herself, he worked out she would have been a hundred years old in about 1989. He wondered if the internet had even existed in 1989 and considered, realistically, the chances of her having lived so long would have been slim – given all her health problems and the lack of medical care back then. He also remembered, fondly, her desire for success and her wish to be a doctor.

Taking a chance, he typed in: "Doctor Charlotte Simmonds, born 1889."

And then he saw it. Half way down the page there was an entry for an old BBC documentary on "Important Women in Medicine" which had a link to: "Doctor Charlotte Simmonds, a woman of her time." It was being shown on BBC iplayer as part of a tribute to 2018 being a hundred years from when women were given the vote for the first time. Eddie was astonished, for a moment, that there had been a time when women were not allowed to vote.

There was a small picture of an old woman, with grey hair and brown eyes smiling into the camera. He clicked on the link with shaking hands and it led him to a BBC clip from 1990. Nearly thirty years ago, but, thanks to the wonders of the internet, available for him to watch on his computer here and now.

Surely this couldn't be her, she would have been 101 years old. Trembling, he clicked the play button.

The elderly woman was sitting sideways on, talking to another, younger, lady who was interviewing her. They were both
dressed in modern, but slightly old-fashioned clothes. The film
was slightly grainy and not as clear as the programmes on the
TV nowadays.

Eddie peered closely at the screen, trying to recognise something in the older woman, anything that could link her back to
that young girl, with ribbons in her hair and a white smock. Her
voice was thin but clear and she was talking gently about her
world-renowned career in medicine and her ground-breaking
work on the treatment of asthma.

"It was difficult for girls in my day," she told the interviewer.
"I had to fight to stay at school as a teacher's helper as my parents wanted me to help them in their bakery. But I managed
to persuade them and I stayed on, helping the younger children
and eventually becoming a teacher myself. I had a lot of health
problems as a child and struggled badly with asthma from a
young age. I always had a desire to do something with medicine
and help both myself and other people. I suppose my own ex-
periences with asthma were what led to my research into that
illness.

"Then the First World War happened, which was a terrible,
terrible time, but which also allowed me to train as a nurse. I
spent many months working with wounded soldiers near the
battlefields of France. What I saw there will never leave me. But
it also made me more determined than ever.

"After the war, things were very different for women. We
were suddenly needed as so many men had been killed. I managed to continue in my career as a nurse and then studied to be a
medical doctor. There were a lot of people who thought women
should stay at home and look after their children, so I never
married but concentrated on what I loved – medicine.

"I had a fabulous career, working abroad in America where
women doctors were more accepted than they were here. I
came home and worked for a time at St Mary's Hospital in Lon-
don, in the research lab of Alexander Fleming. I remember talk-

ing to him about his new discovery, which eventually led to the development of antibiotics – probably one of the greatest medical advances in history. Infections that had killed people in the past would be treatable and not nearly as dangerous as they had been. That was probably the highlight of my career, for very personal reasons. I talked with Alexander about how his new discovery could be used in medicine, but he didn't realise how important it would be and went on to research other things. The huge steps forward in antibiotics were left to others to take."

Eddie's eyes grew wide. If this was, indeed, Charlotte, he had given her those antibiotics, so she had already known how this medicine would change the world. He could imagine her trying to persuade the famous Alexander Fleming that his discovery could, and would, change the world.

"And what were those reasons?" asked the interviewer, nodding to her in encouragement.

"Well," said the old lady. "I am getting old now and my body is frail, although my mind is as clear as ever."

She smiled warmly at the interviewer, the lines around her eyes and mouth deep and worn.

"A long time ago a young friend visited me. This person was kind, brave and generous. He gave me a great gift, which saved my life. He was a boy who predicted how different life was going to be for me in the future.

"My career in medicine finished in my early seventies, but I saw how computers started to change things and I have kept in touch with my former, younger colleagues. I have seen incredible things happening thanks to this new technology and I have huge hopes for what will happen in the future. But I also now know that this new world is going to be full of new kinds of challenges, some good and some bad. I suppose I am hoping to send this boy a message."

"A message? Do you think he is still alive? He would surely be very old by now," questioned the other, younger woman, thinking, of course, that the old lady was talking about someone who had lived decades ago in her own time.

"He will be and, you never know, he might even one day see this film and hear my message," said the older woman. Only Eddie could understand what she meant by those three words: 'he will be'.

"Because," she continued firmly, "I want to tell him I now know what his magic box is, and maybe he will use it to find this programme - although I am not sure how. My last message must be to him."

She turned to face the camera, almost as if she had planned it. It was as though the whole interview was about this one moment. Her brown eyes twinkled through her frail, aged skin, and Eddie knew at once that it was her.

"I just want to say, thank you Eddie, from across the stories of time."

The presenter looked slightly puzzled, clearly thinking the old lady was showing some confusion, which the younger woman probably put down to her age. The interview carried on, discussing Charlotte's many achievements, and then moved on to interview two other women who had done great things in medicine. Eddie watched it all, transfixed.

As the credits started to roll at the end, a few words appeared across the black background.

In memory of Dr Charlotte Simmonds
Born 1889, died 1990 aged 101.

CHAPTER 40

The day of the exhibition opening at the museum drew closer. The organisers had told Eddie that he could take along a couple of friends from the school, as well as his mum. He had asked Alfie and Ethan to come along with him and they jumped at the chance.

"Do you think they will give us sweets?" asked Ethan, his teeth enthusiastically biting over his bottom lip in expectation of some delicious treats.

"Oh, do be quiet," said Alfie. "This is a serious event, not some sort of sweet shop."

"But people always give kids sweets at things like that," protested Ethan, swiping at Alfie.

Eddie watched them, happy that they were his friends and feeling pretty good about himself.

His mother was beside herself with excitement and had used some of her recent pay packet to buy a new dress for the occasion. She had managed to keep hold of her job at Tesco Express, despite having to take a day off due to Eddie being suspended. She had come downstairs to show her son her new outfit and he had to admit, she looked pretty good in a smart woollen, dress which brushed stylishly against her knees. She was also wearing a pair of new shoes with small heels. Eddie gave her the thumbs-up and said: "I am proud of you too, mum." Her face flushed in delight as she scuttled over to him and gave him a quick hug.

"My famous writer, that's what you are," she whispered into

his ear.

Eddie had thought a lot about the film he had watched on the internet. He had asked Mrs Jameson at school about when the internet had been invented and she had said she wasn't really sure, so they had looked it up together one lunchtime. It was actually pretty complicated, but Mrs Jameson tried to make some sense of it.

"So, computer systems had been developing since the 1960s," she said, squinting at her screen.

"But it was in 1990 that a British computer scientist called Tim Berners-Lee invented what was known as the world wide web. That eventually became what we call the internet – where people could access and share information all over the world."

He liked his teacher. She always had time for his many questions and was happy to spend parts of her lunchtime talking to and encouraging him.

"Pretty keen on the internet are you?" she asked, turning away from her screen and looking at him.

"Yes," he answered. "I would like to be someone like that man, Tim ....."

"Berners-Lee," she reminded him, glancing back at the information on her computer. "A computer scientist."

"Someone told me once I was a famous writer," said Eddie. "But I actually think I want to be a computer scientist when I grow up."

"That sounds like a wonderful ambition," said his teacher, with a note of warning in her voice. "But remember, the internet is full of both wonders and dangers. Never forget that."

Eddie went outside to see his friends. His mind went over and over how Charlotte had spoken in the BBC film. She must have realised that she was at the end of her full and adventurous life and was thinking back to those momentous events when she was just a young girl attending a small village school.

She was clever and a scientist herself and must have realised that the computers were Eddie's magic box. She never lived to see the internet sweep its influence through the world, but she obviously had an idea of what was to come.

Although she was very old, her mind was still bright and active and she was able to make the connection and send out that incredible message through time; in a film that Eddie could maybe one day discover. Luck had played a huge part in him finding it, but Charlotte's message had managed to stubbornly tunnel itself through the years and find the person it was intended for. Eddie. The thought filled him with admiration for her and astonishment that indeed she had remembered him until she was a hundred years old. She had reached out for him in the future through time, as he had reached out to her in the past.

The day of the museum prize-giving arrived. Eddie and his mum drove to pick up Alfie and Ethan, who were all smartly dressed in their school uniforms, with bright red jumpers and long grey trousers as the wintry weather was now cold and wet.

Eddie and his mum had spent some time cleaning the house the previous evening so that it was "nice to come home to". She was still a little pleasantly surprised by Eddie's occasional efforts to help out with tidying his room and doing the washing up. And he had given her a big smile that morning when she came downstairs looking elegant in her newly-bought outfit.

Dozens of people packed the exhibition hall, which had displays of work from all the schools in the area.

There were also boards of information produced by the museum about how children lived in the past, displaying facts about the Anglo Saxons, Tudors and the two world wars.

Eddie and his friends wandered through them, looking at examples of paintings, photographs and even real-life artefacts which helped illustrate the information the museum historians had gathered together. It must have taken a huge amount of work.

Eddie's mum was drinking orange juice ("such a shame I have to drive!") and chatting to Mrs Jameson, who was representing the school, on the other side of the room.

And there, in the middle of all the bustle and chatter, on a huge white board, was Eddie's story. It had been beautifully produced, with each word clearly printed and a large photograph of Eddie next to it. He stood in front of it, next to his two friends, and glowed with pride.

Around it was a display on "Victorian children in the Fordingham area" with many photographs, examples of Victorian toys and clothes, and even copies of entries from real-life log books from schools in the area which dated back to Victorian times. So much information and history, yet Eddie knew more than all of them what life was like in reality for those children who had lived so long ago.

"Wow," said Ethan, impressed. "That board with your writing on it is almost as big as me!" Eddie laughed a little and shrugged.

"Aw, it's a bit embarrassing really," he said, a little untruthfully.

Miss Downing appeared behind them and spoke quietly to Eddie.

"Are you ready, young man?" she said, a smile in her voice. "It's time for the presentation."

Eddie nodded at her and his two friends wandered off to the group of adults, which included the Mayor with his furry cornered hat, scarlet robes and a huge gold medallion chain around his neck.

Just about to join them, Eddie's eyes were caught by a photograph pinned to a display about schools in the villages around Fordingham.

He moved closer to it as a hush descended on the busy clatter around him as people organised themselves for the exhibition launch and the presentation of Eddie's prize.

He moved right up to the black and white photograph in the middle, which had obviously been enlarged for the exhibition. It was surprisingly clear and every little detail had been preserved.

It was of a group of children, about ten years old, all standing in lines with a stern-looking teacher standing in the middle. Her hair was scraped back into a bun and she had small, metal-rimmed glasses on the end of her nose.

The girls were standing on one side and the boys on the other. The hand-written title underneath said "St Paul's School, Stoneham Cross, Summer 1899".

He moved even closer, his heart dancing and thumping with excitement.

For there, in the middle, next to the teacher, was a girl with shoulder-length, brown hair, tied back with white ribbons, and a long white smock. Her face was thin, but she was smiling happily and confidently at the camera. She looked like she was preparing to take on the world. Charlotte.

EPILOGUE

I t was two weeks after the prize-giving and Eddie was sitting in his bedroom, holding a small package. The box was wrapped in shiny, silver paper and finished off with a scarlet ribbon tied into a bow with curls tumbling away down the sides.

He looked down at the object in his hands and remembered how after school he had asked Mrs Hall, Alfie's mum, to help him with a plan. Eddie's mother had not yet arrived to pick him up so he had grabbed the chance to explain what he was planning to do and Mrs Hall had instantly agreed to help, giving him a quick hug and a beaming smile.

His mum arrived a few moments later, and Mrs Hall asked her if Eddie could come around, again, the following day for tea. His mum agreed cheerfully, commenting how nice it was for Eddie to have "such lovely friends".

But instead of going straight to Alfie's house, the three of them, Eddie clasping his £100 prize in his hands, had carried on down the High

Street towards a small shop. Eddie had been wandering through the shops the previous weekend with his mother, looking in the windows and, when he had seen it, he had known exactly how he was going to spend his money.

And here he was, in his bedroom, with the package in his hands and his heart pounding with a mixture of excitement and nerves. He had never done anything like this before.

Holding the box, beautifully wrapped by the shop assistant, he took a deep breath and went downstairs. His mother was in the kitchen, peeling the plastic cover off the pizza they were having for dinner.

Eddie looked at her from the doorway as she hummed quietly to herself, pushing away her hair with the back of her hand.

Sensing he was there, she turned and smiled at him.

"Ready in fifteen minutes!" she said cheerfully, placing the plastic in the bin and opening the oven door before putting the pizza in.

"Mum," said Eddie, quietly. "I have got something for you."

His mother stopped midway in the kitchen and looked over at him, his serious tone of voice worrying her a little.

Eddie walked over to her and placed the small package on the table.

"I got you this," he muttered, awkwardly.

She looked at him in surprise and walked hesitantly over to the package, turning it around in her hands and admiring the paper and ribbon.

"What is it?" she asked.

"Open it and see," said Eddie encouragingly.

So she carefully unwrapped the box, placing the ribbon and paper on the table and stroking the velvet box inside. She looked at her son questioningly and then slowly lifted the lid.

Inside, glistening and sparkling on the black cloth, was a silver chain draped over a soft little cushion. And resting on the plump velvet was a little silver hourglass with tiny, glimmering grains of sand.

She gasped with delight and touched the necklace gently. And she instantly knew how he had paid for it.

With tears in her eyes, her hands shaking with emotion, she folded her son in a big, warm hug.

"Eddie, you are the kindest boy in the world," she said.

As the dust settled into the nooks and crannies of St Paul's Primary School, the daylight was squeezed from the evening sky.

The cleaners shut the doors, set the alarms and left the school silent and empty.

A strange blue light suddenly shimmered and flickered around the little brown door, as if stroking it lovingly. The light sharpened into a bright line and concentrated on the handle, ringing it faster and faster with circles of blue stripes.

All at once, the glare disappeared. The corridor was left in near darkness, the silver of the door's handle glinting a little through the gloom.

And there, with its top part full of sand waiting to tip into the empty chamber below, was an hourglass decorated with swirls and stars.

First of all, thank you for purchasing Time's Running Out for Eddie Watson. I know you could have picked any number of books to read, but you picked this book and for that I am extremely grateful.

I hope that it added at value and quality to your everyday life. If so, it would be really nice if you could share this book with your friends and family by posting to Facebook and Twitter.

If you enjoyed this book and found some benefit in reading this, I'd like to hear from you and hope that you could take some time to post a review on Amazon. Your feedback and support will help this author to greatly improve her writing craft for future projects and make this book even better.

I want you, the reader, to know that your review is very important and so, if you'd like to leave a review, all you have to do is go to the Amazon page for this book and post away! I wish you all the best in your future success!

Printed in Great
Britain
by Amazon